'You and I need to talk,' Tom said quietly, not looking at her.

Harriet tried not to gulp. 'Mr and Mrs Atkinson can tell you everything you need to know. It's quite simple.'

'You know I don't mean that.' He stabbed the desk with his pen. 'Stop playing this stupid game with me.'

'I'm not playing any game,' Harry hissed, backing away.

'Then why,' he stepped towards her, 'did you try to avoid me just now? I saw you about to sneak away.' He reached out and took her by the wrist, and she felt his fingers burning her flesh like hot metal. 'We're going to have to learn to work together, whether you like if or not. That's why I want to talk to you.'

'The way you talked to me once before?'

Holly North was born in Cambridge in 1955. She read History at Durham University and 1978 married her American husband, Sam. His career has taken them all over the world, from New York and Paris to Saudi Arabia and Japan. Holly teaches English and restores oriental carpets when she can—and when she can't, she keeps herself sane by writing about her home country. She's a passionate advocate of the NHS, which looks all the more impressive from abroad, and consults her brother-in-law, who is a paediatrician, for much of the medical detail in her books.

Holly North has written five other Doctor and Nurse Romances; her previous titles include *Nurse at Large, Dr Malone, I Presume?* and *Invisible Doctor*.

To C. S. of Great Ormond Street with thanks for advice and information.

RESORTING TO MAGIC

BY

HOLLY NORTH

MILLS & BOON LIMITED
ETON HOUSE   18-24 PARADISE ROAD
RICHMOND   SURREY   TW9 1SR

First published in Great Britain 1989 by Mills & Boon Limited

© Holly North 1989

Australian copyright 1989 Philippine copyright 1989 This edition 1989

ISBN 0 263 76483 4

Set in English Times 10 on 11½ pt. 03 – 8907 – 57432

Typeset in Great Britain by JCL Graphics, Bristol

Made and Printed in Great Britain

CHAPTER ONE

HARRIET Hart swung back the doors of Paddington Ward and reeled, as she did every morning, at the din. She could pick out the various components that made it up as surely as she could have identified the sounds of an orchestra. In the rhythm section was the persistent and unceasing wail of a small child. On top of that was imposed the blare of the television set and the bleeping of a computer game which had been brought in for one of the patients as a gift and was slowly driving the staff mad. And then there were the hundred and one noisy activities of a busy children's ward—a nursery-rhyme singalong led by one of the parents, the thudding echo of a plastic ball being bounced across the floor, the jangle of a medicine trolley being wheeled around and the overlying pattern of children's voices and footsteps as they ran around. From the noise they made, you'd never guess they were ill, Harry thought.

She walked down the hallway, past the three rooms where the parents could stay overnight, the treatment room, and Sister O'Brien's office. Stuck to the door of the office was a large picture of some terrible monster with three legs, green hair and a purple nose, like that of a hardened alcoholic. Underneath, written in large, wobbly handwriting were the words 'Sitser Pat'.

The entrance area opened on to the main section of Paddington Ward, its walls covered in Paddington Bear wallpaper and the beds and cots divided by brightly coloured curtains. At the end of the ward, out of sight but not beyond hearing, were the playroom and the television-room. A turn to the right led through another set of doors and into Rupert Ward, where the children who needed peace and quiet stayed until they were ready to face Paddington. The paediatric unit was completed by Teddy Ward, where sick babies and infants were treated. To get there one had to go back out of Paddington and down the main corridor.

Harry loved it—the noise, the bustle, the informality, everything about it. Each day when she walked in she realised once more that in choosing to specialise in paediatrics she made the right decision. Others had thought her crazy; after all, it was tough enough surviving the years as an ordinary houseman, let alone getting through all that and then volunteering for another stint in a junior post just so that she could do her paediatric training. But even after two years, no matter how exhausted she felt, Paddington Ward could always cheer her. Working here was like being surrounded by one big family.

She looked around for Sister O'Brien, but before she could locate her a little girl dressed in a scarlet jumper and skirt came tearing over. 'Dr Harry!' Harry bent down and scooped her up, settling her comfortably on one hip.

'Oooh, you're getting heavy!' she groaned, taking the strain. 'Now. What's all the fuss about, Mandy?'

'My mummy's coming . . . I'm going to see my granny this afternoon . . . and then I can go back to play school . . .' Mandy spluttered.

'That sounds good,' said Harry non-committally. She

spotted Pat O'Brien bent over the files at the nurses' station and carried Mandy over, asking, 'But what about your operation? Have you forgotten about that?'

'I'm not having it,' said the child firmly.

Sister Pat looked up and smiled. She was small, auburn-haired and famed for her combination of a soft heart and a hard head. 'Good morning. You're early today,' she observed.

'I thought I'd do my round before this new consultant arrives; we don't want to look as if we're slacking, do we?' Harry said wryly. She was responsible for most of the routine work on the ward, and any backlog could be laid directly at her door.

There was another reason for being so conscientious—though she hadn't admitted it to anyone else. The new man was a specialist in childhood cancer and serious diseases. At the moment, all complicated cases, and most of their paediatric cancer cases, were transferred to another hospital with a special unit. But with the arrival of the new doctor they would be treating them here, at St Hugh's. The new consultant would need a registrar, and the registrar would need a houseman. And Harry was determined to fill one or the other of the posts. Going for the registrar's job was pretty ambitious, she knew. After all, she was only twenty-seven and they usually didn't look at you until you were pushing thirty. But there was no reason at all why she couldn't be his houseman. It was just a matter of hitting it off with him and then engineering the transfer. At that moment Mandy kicked her and roused her from her momentary lapse of concentration.

'What's this Mandy's been telling me about not having an operation?' Harry asked.

'Oh, that's the good news. Wait till you see what we've got.' Pat disappeared into the small office behind the nurses' desk, then returned clutching a clear plastic bag. Inside, when Harry looked, was a small plastic model from a breakfast cereal packet. 'We can't tell whether it's Darth Vader or Luke Skywalker—but anyway, it made its appearance yesterday evening in the natural way,' Pat explained.

'Clever girl.' Harry gave her patient a hug. 'So your Mum was right—you did swallow it after all. And now you won't have to have that operation on your tum. Your Mum's going to be very pleased.'

'Can you do some magic?' asked Mandy.

Harry pretended to think about it for a moment. 'Well . . . ' She bunched her fingers and made a fist, opened her hand to reveal that nothing was there, closed her fingers and blew on them, then put her hand to the clild's ear and said in surprise, 'What this you've got in your ear? Oh, look, a sweet!' Using sleight of hand she pretended to pull the sweet from the little girl's ear; the child reached out and took it and Harry lowered her to the ground, where she ran off to show her friends.

Pat O'Brien watched. She'd seen it all before. 'You'd better be careful,' she said, a trace of her original Irish lilt still detectable. 'One day you'll forget to put those sweets in your pocket and there'll be a riot in this ward.'

Harry grinned. The trick had taught to her by one of her old tutors at medical school, years ago. At the time she'd thought it was a bit silly, now she appreciated that it worked *real* magic on frightened or nervous children.

'We've had Mandy in for observation for fourteen days,' she mused, looking through the case notes Pat had placed on the desk. 'That must be some sort of record. I was beginning to think her mother had made a mistake and Darth Vader was just tucked down the back of the sofa. At least we didn't have to operate, that's the main thing.' She handed back the file. 'Perhaps you could call her mother and suggest that she picks Mandy up after lunch—that should give us time to discharge her.'

Pat nodded and made a note.

'Mandy was the good news—who's the bad?' Harry asked.

'Damian Potter.' Sister made his name sound like a rude word. 'As you'll no doubt remember, last week he tried to run away when the playleader took a group of the kids down to the hospital shop for sweets. And he made another escape attempt last night. According to the night staff he got as far as the car-park. Fortunately someone from Casualty was outside having a cigarette and they spotted him and brought him back.' She nodded towards the bed nearest the nurses' station where Damian lay glowering at them from under the bedclothes. 'The first time was amusing but now it's getting beyond a joke. I really don't have enough staff to keep a non-stop watch on him.'

'I appreciate that,' Harry murmured, but it was difficult to be furious with Damian. He was naughty, but he also had the mischievous charm of every bright eight-year-old. However, running away was a serious problem. In her mind's eye Harry could imagine the newspaper headlines— Damian Potter, supposed to be tucked up safe and sound in hospital, found wandering in his pyjamas in west London in the early hours of the morning. Or, worse still, run over, or abducted or murdered by a maniac.

'We've confiscated his pyjama trousers,' said Pat, her eyes twinkling, 'so that should put the kybosh on him. Although he's already tried to bribe one of the younger children to smuggle him a spare pair. We'll just have to watch him like a hawk.'

'And I need to check Kirsty Hill's cannula again,' Harry remembered. 'While I'm at it I might as well remove Sanjay's drainage tube, if you can spare me a nurse.' She reached for the green cards in the rack at the side of the desk. 'I also want four blood tests on the little girl who was admitted to Rupert yesterday. She's to stay in quarantine until we're quite sure she hasn't got measles.'

Pat nodded and went off to find a nurse, while Harry fished her pen from her pocket and began to fill out the blood test cards. It took several minutes to fill in the details. She signed them all quickly and popped them into the box on the desk—and as she looked up, out of the corner of her eyes she spotted Damian Potter, clad in his pyjama jacket and with a towel wrapped round his waist, slipping out of the main ward.

'Oh, no, you don't, Damian!' Pocketing her pen, she made a dash after him—but at that moment one of the auxiliary nurses emerged from the linen-room with a trolley piled with clean sheets and wheeled it right across her path. It gave Damian the few seconds he needed, and in the time it took Harry to negotiate the trolley he'd disappeared, leaving the ward door swinging behind him.

'Blast!' she looked around. Apart from the startled auxiliary there was no one about. She'd have to go after him herself. By the time she reached the corridor, he had a fifteen-metre start. What's more, his bare feet gripped the freshly polished white floor tiles, while her leather-soled court shoes kept skidding as if she was running on ice. With growing frustration she realised that if she wasn't careful the little scamp would actually get away from her. 'Stop him!' she yelled.

It was still early and there were very few people in sight. An elderly gentleman heading for the physiotherapy department with his walking frame made a brave attempt to block the child's path, but Damian just ducked and squeezed through. Harry lost ground again as she carefully edged past the old chap's Zimmer frame.

Then Damian made a tactical error. Instead of turning right, which would have taken him to the main entrance hall, he turned left, in the direction of the offices and staff rooms used by the medical staff. PRIVATE, read the sign above the corridor. Off each side were lots of little turnings, most of them, Harry knew, dead ends.

Damian took another sharp left, Harry in hot pursuit. She was almost within grabbing distance of him now when he swerved suddenly to the right, round another corner. Harry made a lunge and caught the towel—which came away in her hand. But even the fact that he was now half-naked didn't deter Damian and he headed onwards in the direction of the consultant's offices. Her eyes fixed on his bare bottom, just waiting for the right moment to pounce, Harry followed. As he approached one door it opened; he paused for a split second and then decided to dash in. Harry lunged again. 'Now I've got you, you little rascal!' she crowed, managing to catch him for a second. Then he wriggled and kicked, throwing her off balance. She tripped forward, and at the same moment the doorway was blocked by a tall figure. As she stretched out her arms to save herself, her hands encountered something firm and soft and warm, and suspiciously like a man's thigh—then she cannoned into him.

What happened next she wasn't sure. He must somehow have scooped her up, just milliseconds before she hit the ground. At any rate, she found herself pressed full-length against him, her cheek hard against his chest, one strong arm clasping her firmly. She could feel her legs, weak-kneed with exertion, tangled with his, her breasts pressed against his ribcage. And she could also, most disconcertingly, sense the fresh-soaped male smell of him and feel his breath in her hair. Time seemed to stand still as she fought for a lungful of air. She couldn't somehow swallow; she couldn't move. She seemed to have become absorbed in this peculiarly intimate embrace—and he held her just a second longer that was absolutely necessary. There was complete silence.

Then, suddenly, she seemed to regain her breath and her equilibrum. Who on earth was it, holding her in his arms like this? Not her boss, Philip Beech, who was scarcely her own height and couldn't possibly have lifted her up so easily. Not old Stanley Medway, the consultant urologist. Not even Guy Parkinson, who was widely reckoned to be the best-looking consultant physician in the hospital. It took a split second for her to run through and then eliminate all the other possibilities. None of the St Hugh's consultants measured up to the man who was now gently releasing her from his arms. Flustered, she put her hands to his chest and found them welded there by some strange, warm force. She pulled them away, not daring to look up at him, for she knew she must be pink-cheeked with confusion.

'I'm sorry. Are you all right?' she muttered. Then she remembered Damian. 'Did you see where he went? He's run away from the paediatric ward and I was chasing him.'

'He's in here.' The man turned sideways in the doorway so that she could see Damian sitting, feigning wide-eyed innocence, on one of the chairs, his lap modestly covered with a copy of *The Lancet*.

'Damian, you're the absolute limit. Why do you keep running away?' Harry scolded, holding out the towel. 'Go on, put this on and we'll go back to Paddington Ward.'

Her composure almost restored, she turned back to the man and smiled. 'Thanks for catching me. I might have done myself a nasty injury if . . .' The words froze on her tongue as for the first time she took in his face—the dark, almost black hair, the eyes that were the same heartstopping blue as the brilliant sea around a Greek island. Perhaps it was just a coincidence, she thought for a fleeting moment—but no, no one else could possibly share that face. No one else could have that profile, that jaw. And he was so tall, just as she remembered. She was just four inches short of six feet herself, but she only came up to his shoulder. Above all, no other man could possess that indefinable but overwhelming aura of power. Her response to it came flooding back, an echo from the past.

The first time she'd met him she'd been stunned by his sheer physical magnetism. She'd been like a rabbit hypnotised by a car's headlights—too dazzled to realise what was happening. And when she *had* realised what was going on, it was too late to escape.

But now there was a difference. That first time she hadn't been prepared for him. Now she was. She knew what he was really like. She'd thought about him more than she liked to admit. And she'd always wondered how she'd react if she ever met him again. In her dreams she had squashed him with a barbed put-down or a single look. Now, face to face with the real man, it was different. '*You*,' was all she could say, and it came out in a whisper. 'What are *you* doing here?' But there was no mistaking the animosity in her voice.

For a split second he showed his surprise. Then he clamped down and studied her with narrowed eyes. Who the hell was she? Her face seemed suddenly familiar—but how could he have forgotten her? He'd just been admiring her long dark hair, worn in a topknot, and her square-jawed face and well-defined cheekbones. No one would have called her classically beautiful, but there was something serene-looking about her. He glanced down at her slim legs, visible beneath a skirt that stopped an inch above her knees—feminine, and fashionable, yet discreet and smart. He refrained from any sign of approval.

She obviously knew him—but how? Had they worked together? He felt sure he would have remembered her. Perhaps they had trained together? No, she was too young. Judging from her tone of voice, she wasn't pleased to see him. An unpleasant thought occurred to him. Had they been out together? Had something gone wrong? He couldn't believe he would have forgotten her.

Then an image suddenly came to him. A shabby room—a student's room, with posters tacked to the walls and a kelim rug covered in holes on the floor. And a pretty sleepy girl with short dark hair and face as pale as a ghost's. She'd been wearing a blue kimono, and she'd had the look and smell of a freshly bathed child, just ready for bed. It came back to him as vividly as if it had been yesterday. He winced at the memory, which he had hoped would never be revived. There were very few moments of his life he regretted, but the half-hour he'd spent with this girl was one of them.

'Harriet Hart.' He said it slowly. Her name seemed to come to him from the past.

'And you're Tom Buchanan,' she said, with a little acknowledging nod.

'You're working here?'

'I'm a houseman on Paediatrics,' she admitted matter-of-factly. The memory of that night he'd come to visit her had returned so clearly that she could feel the same mixture of shock and helpless anger she had felt then. It was irrational, she knew, but you couldn't wipe the past away. He'd made an indelible impact. He'd been part of her life—part of her.

Now he looked at her steadily, trying to gauge her reaction to what he had to say next. 'I'm in paediatrics too. In fact I've just joined the staff. I've come to set up . . .'

'I can guess,' said Harry blankly. 'I know about the new cancer unit. I just hadn't been told your name. If I had . . .'

He gave the slightest of smiles. 'What would you have done?'

Harry tried to think of the right thing to say, unaware of the fact that she was suddenly as pale as she had been that night six years ago when he had erupted equally unexpectedly into her life. Maybe she should congratulate him, laugh and say 'let bygones be bygones', but she had too much pride for that. Or maybe she should be devastatingly rude—and then go and hand in her notice, because if Tom Buchanan was going to be working on the paediatric team, she didn't want to be a part of it. Or maybe she should just pretend that she'd forgotten what had happened. Discretion, she decided, was the better part of valour. 'Nothing,' she said cagily. But he couldn't miss the fact that she was less than thrilled to see him.

Damian, as if sensing the electricity, gave a loud sigh. 'Come on,' said Harry, turning to him, 'back to Paddington Ward.' And she took him by the hand, and the back of the pyjama jacket for good measure, and led him past the new consultant into the corridor.

'Harriet, I'd like to . . .' She turned, tight-lipped, and he saw the sudden flash of fear and anger in her eyes.

'Nothing,' he said, echoing her own evasion. The apologetic smile that had frozen on his face seemed to transform itself into a sneer.

Harriet led Damian back to the ward, her thoughts grey. The doors swung shut behind them, but for once all the noise and the activity didn't lift her spirits. It was impossible to believe that everything had been right with the world, but in the space of a few minutes a tall shadow had fallen over her.

'What's the problem?' asked Pat O'Brien, seeing her long face.

'No problem,' Harry responded. But there was. The problem was called Tom Buchanan—and the trouble was only just beginning.

'But what did he *do*?' asked Steve Paige in exasperation.

'You keep telling me what an awful man he is, but *why*? What's he done? It must be something pretty terrible.'

Harry turned to check that the door of their office was firmly shut. She could trust Steve. They had worked together as housemen on the paediatric unit ever since she'd come to St Hugh's—but she didn't want anyone else to overhear. She didn't have many close friends because there simply hadn't been enough time to make them, but working and worrying and panicking together on Paddington Ward had established a good bond between the pair of them.

'It wasn't terrible. It was just something very unfair.' Harry closed her eyes for a second. 'And it's something that I've never been able to forget.'

'Look,' Steve butted in, shuffling papers all the while, 'if you don't get to the point quickly I'll have to go. I've got Outpatients in ten minutes.'

'All right,' Harry muttered. 'Years ago—I'm not sure, it must be about six—when I was at medical school, I went out with his younger brother, Alex Buchanan. He was a medical student too.' Harry shook her head. 'I must have been mad to have had anything to do with him. I was very serious about it all, the model student, hanging on the consultants' every word—all that sort of thing. Alex was really just there for the social life. His family were very well off and he had no problems with money like the rest of us. While I was working he just drank a lot and went out with hundreds of nurses and in between times tried to avoid killing any of his patients.'

'Everyone's image of the classic student doctor,' Steve said witheringly. 'If only they knew! But how did a swot like you get involved with him?'

Harry winced with embarrassment. 'As I said, I must have been mad. There I was, being so conscientious, never going out, never having fun. And the one time I was persuaded to go to a party and had a couple of glasses of wine, I ended up dancing with him.'

'So young and innocent,' observed Steve drily.

'Well, I *was*,' spluttered Harry. 'I didn't approve of the kind of things he did. But he was fun, and I hadn't had much fun for a long time. He had a kind of glamour about him that it's difficult to resist when you're just out of your teens. He had a sports car, too, an MGB GT, which I liked the look of.'

'True confessions!' Steve chuckled. 'Women—so easily impressed by a heap of rust on wheels.'

Harry ignored him. 'Anyway, we went out a few times . . .' Steve gave a mocking tut-tut. 'Look, I'm not going to apologise for it,' she said defensively. 'Everyone's allowed to go off the rails once when they're young. It wasn't anything serious—at least, it wasn't as far as I was concerned.'

'So what happened to change things?'

'Nothing much. After a few weeks I began to get bored with sitting around while he and his flashy friends drank themselves silly. The car kept breaking down, too. Finals were coming up and one of my tutors gave me a big lecture about how, if I wasn't careful, I'd throw away my chances of a decent career—and anyhow, I began to realise that I'd got Alex out of my system. I didn't actually like him very much once I got to know him. He was very selfish. He did whatever he wanted to do, and I wasn't allowed any say in it. So I just——'

'Gave him the elbow?' suggested Steve. Harry

nodded. 'Very wise. Forgive me for being stupid,' he continued, 'but where does Big Brother Buchanan come into all this?'

Harry went pink. 'After I'd told Alex I wasn't going to see him again I went home for the weekend.' She paused. 'Actually I didn't tell him, I wrote him a note and then I ran for cover. He liked having things his own way, and I didn't want a row. And besides, I didn't think he was very serious about me. I still don't think he was.'

Steve looked at his watch. 'You've got four minutes to finish the story, then I'll have to go.'

Harry raised her hands. 'OK. I got back to the hall of residence on the Sunday evening. There was no note or anything from Alex. I went to bed. At midnight there was a knock at the door.'

'Alex?'

'No, a man I'd never seen before. He introduced himself as Tom Buchanan, Alex's brother. I was a bit thrown—he's not the sort of man . . . Well, you'll see for yourself, sooner or later. He's not a man you can ignore or say no to. He's very forceful.' She swallowed. 'I was half-asleep, so I let him in. The next thing I knew, he was yelling at me, demanding why I'd ditched Alex in such a shabby manner. He kept going on about how could I have done it when I knew how much I meant to Alex. I didn't understand what he was talking about. And then he told me about the accident.'

'At last this is beginning to get interesting,' commented Steve. 'Keep going.'

Harry put her hand to her brow. 'This is the first time I've told anyone about it. It's not exactly a secret, it was just such a mess . . .'

'It's safe with me,' promised Steve. 'Only tell me quickly, or I'll be in suspense all afternoon.'

Harry rubbed her eyes. To Steve it might seem something of a joke, but to her it was serious. 'Eventually, he told me what had happened—or the Buchanan version of it, anyway. Apparently Alex had got my note and been so upset—at least, that was what he'd said—that he'd gone out drinking. Then he'd decided to drive down to my parents' place. He had an accident on the M4 near Chippenham.'

'He was killed?'

'No!' Harry pulled an aghast face. 'Nothing as bad as that. Compound fractures to both legs, a couple of crushed ribs and some minor contusions. He was lucky.'

'So why was Big Brother hopping mad?'

'Lots of reasons, including the fact that a little girl in the back of the car Alex hit had her back broken.'

'And Big Brother is a paediatrician . . . No wonder he was mad.'

'It gets worse,' Harry said flatly. 'Alex was charged with drunken driving. For a while they thought the girl was going to die—in which case he could have been up for manslaughter. But the final insult, as far as Tom was concerned, was that Alex wasn't going to be able to sit his Finals.'

'And it was all your fault.' Steve said it so matter-of-factly that Harry went white.

There was a strained silence. 'So you think so, too, do you?' Harry said at last, her voice hollow.

'Of course not!' Steve protested. 'But I can see that Alex might have wanted to make it look that way.'

Harry shrugged agreement. 'He'd told the police and

his brother that we were about to get engaged when I'd walked out on him without a word of explanation. He made it sound as if I was some sort of heartless bitch after his money. And *he* ended up sounding like a romantic hero—so desperately in love that he couldn't stop himself drinking and then getting in his car. What do they call it in France? A crime of passion?' She clenched her fists. 'Anyway, I didn't know all this at the time. All I knew was that this huge, furious man had burst into my room and started accusing me of all kinds of things. He kept telling me that I'd ruined Alex's career; he called me every name under the sun. He even threatened to get me thrown out of college so that *I* couldn't take my Finals either . . .' She stopped. Steve had begun to laugh. 'It wasn't funny, Steve.'

Steve wiped his eyes with the back of his hand. 'Not at the time, maybe, but look at it now. Harry, you mustn't take this the wrong way, but no one in their right mind could possibly mistake you for some callous *femme fatale*. And surely once anyone had given it more than a few minutes' thought they'd be forced to see that Alex was lying. Anyway,' he added firmly, 'no one could seriously hold you responsible for the accident.'

'But he did.' Harry was white-faced. 'He held me responsible for it all. He went on about how the girl was going to die. Nothing I said made any difference.'

'He must have been in one hell of a state,' said Steve, gathering his notes and files.

'So that makes everything all right in your book, does it?'

'No, of course not.' Steve looked at her strangely. 'Maybe you've never worked yourself up into a rage and said things you didn't mean, but I have. I've heard myself ranting and raving at people, while all the time there's a calm little voice in my head telling me I'm getting it all wrong and making a fool of myself . . .'

'Oh, well, maybe I'm the one who should be apologising, and not him.' Harry folded her arms and stared coolly at Steve.

'You know I don't mean that!' He tapped her on the nose with a cardboard file. 'He certainly sounds like an unreasonable bastard, but everyone's entitled to lose their rag once in a while. Let's just hope neither of us has to have too much to do with him on Paddington.'

He caught the fleeting look of disappointment that crossed Harry's face. 'Ah-ha,' he laughed accusingly. 'So you were looking to join his firm, were you?'

'The thought had crossed my mind, I admit,' Harry confessed. 'But that was before I realised who he was.'

Steve shrugged. 'There's nothing to stop you now, is there? He should be feeling guilty as hell for laying into you like he did, so maybe you'll get the red carpet treatment. Anyway, that's all in the past. You did nothing wrong and so there's nothing to worry about.'

Harry was silent, brooding. There was really no point in brooding. There was really no point in Steve telling her all this. She knew it was true; she'd known it since the day it had happened. But Tom Buchanan had made a great job of removing the guilt from Alex and placing it firmly on her shoulders. And somehow, she just couldn't shake it off. The weight of it lay on her heart, and no matter how often her head told her that it was not her fault, as always her heart continued to rule her feelings. For too many years, her parents had made her feel totally responsible for her young sister, and her chosen work strengthened her feelings that all problems were for her to solve.

Steve glanced at his watch, then got to his feet. 'Look, I'm sorry, I've got to go. I know it must have been very upsetting at the time, but try looking back on it now. He was the one who jumped to the wrong conclusions. He's the one who should be apologising. Perhaps now he's here at St Hugh's you should remind him of how wrong he was.'

There was just one thing wrong with Steve's analysis of the situation, thought Harry as he shut the door behind him. If Alex had been the only one involved in the accident she wouldn't have let it haunt her. But there was the little girl, the innocent victim of his stupidity, confined to a wheelchair for the rest of her life. And there was just one thing Harry felt certain of—if she hadn't written that letter to Alex, that kid might have been running around like a normal child today. And that, more than anything, was what was so difficult to bear.

CHAPTER TWO

'GOT time for a game?' came a shout from across the ward. Harry pulled a weary face at Antony Farrell, a tall, stringy fourteen-year-old, too big for his child-size bed. He was recovering from an operation to repair a cartilege in his leg and had grown bored with the company of the under-twelves who dominated Paddington Ward.

Harry looked at her watch and from her pocket pulled the notepad on which she listed all the things that needed doing. Most of them had been crossed off. 'Come on, then. You'll have to beat me very quickly.' She went to sit on the end of his bed. This was what was so good about working on Paddington. No formality to intimidate the kids, no lectures if you sat on the beds, and playing games with the patients was positively encouraged.

'I'll be black,' said said Antony, setting out the board with astonishing speed.

'You're always black,' complained Harry. 'I'm sure that's why you always win.' She shifted a pawn. Just a couple of moves later he'd taken her bishop. 'Blast, I didn't see that coming.'

'You never learn, do you?' her opponent said cheerfully. 'It's like a battle. You've got to plan your tactics in advance. You can't just play it move by move. You've got to take control of the game.'

'Take control of the game, eh?' Harry shifted her knight and removed one of his from the board. 'How's that?' Maybe that was what she needed to do with Tom Buchanan. At the moment he had everything his own way; he was in charge of the game. But just because he was a consultant and she was a humble houseman, it didn't mean that she couldn't get a few things straight with him. Strategy and tactics, that was what she needed. She had to work out what her goal was, and aim towards that.

'Like I said,' crowed Antony, with an infuriating I-told-you-so expression, 'you never learn.' And with that he captured her queen. Harry gave a rueful grin. The problem was, you never knew when you were in control of the game—at least, not if you were playing with someone who'd had more practice, and was more skilled at getting what they wanted.

'I think,' said Harry, looking at her remaining pieces lying scattered around the board, 'I'm going to have to resign.'

'No, you're not.' The voice came suddenly and unexpectedly from above them. They both looked up—into the blue eyes and amused face of Tom Buchanan. Harry looked down again quickly; she felt that awful dragging panic in her abdomen, like a heavy weight pulling the breath and the energy out of her. 'Do you mind if I join in?' he asked Antony.

'Only if you win,' came the reply. 'You a doctor?'

'That's right.' Tom sat on he bed. 'I'm Tom Buchanan.' There wasn't much room and he settled close to Harry, his arm behind her back, his shoulder pressing and supporting hers.

'Thanks for asking *me* if I mind if you join in,' she

muttered, shifting away from him. In doing so her skirt
rode up an inch or so.

'I always like to help out a colleague in distress,' he
said mildly.

'The only reason I'm in distress,' Harry whispered
defiantly, 'is because of you.'

'You've got nice knees, Harry,' observed Antony,
who'd reached the age when he was beginning to take an
interest in things like that. He was also, thought Harry,
old enough to sense when there was trouble to be stirred
up. 'They're not at all knobbly.'

'No, they're not, are they?' was the comment of the
man behind her.

Harry felt her unease turn to seething fury. How
dared he made such a personal comment—particularly
in front of one of her patients? 'Thank you,' she said
tightly, getting to her feet. 'As you two seem to have hit
it off so well I'll leave you to finish the game. I've got
lots of work to get done.' She turned to Tom. 'As I'm
sure *you* will appreciate, Dr Buchanan.'

He looked up at her with a lazy smile that failed to
hide the steely glint in his eyes. 'There's really no need
to call me that. I'd heard that on Paddington Ward
everyone was on first name terms.'

'They are,' confirmed Antony. 'Sister Pat and Dr
Phil. And Harry and Steve, 'cos they're not very old. I
suppose I should call you Dr Tom.'

'In deference to my extreme old age?' Tom laughed.
'Tom or Dr Tom will do, whichever you prefer.'

'This is all very nice, Dr Buchanan,' said Harry, aware
that she would never have dreamed of speaking to another
consultant, or even a registrar, in the same way, 'but it
doesn't help me finish my ward round. I've got to go.'

'You can't go,' said Antony. 'You started the game so you've got to finish. Tom can help you though.' There was a cheeky glint in his eye that Harry hadn't noticed before.

'Come and sit here. It won't take a minute.' Tom leaned over to the opposite side of the bed and smoothed a space for her. Harry paused. She was behaving very badly. This man was her boss, and right now she was at work. Neither of them had any right to bring their personal feelings about each other on to the ward. It would be professional suicide to do that.

'All right, if you insist.' With a casual shrug, Harry walked round the bed and sat where he had indicated. But she made sure that he didn't catch her eye.

'Move your rook to that pawn,' he instructed, leaning over to point out the move.

Harry hesitated for a moment, then moved her hand to take the piece—at the same second that he reached out for it. Their fingers touched. If it had been anyone else in the world she would just have laughed, but his touch was like an electric shock travelling up her arm and suffusing her with warmth. For some extraordinary reason her heart began to race. She drew her hand back as if scalded. It was unbearable—seeing this man again, speaking to him, *that* was bad enough. But touching him . . . She sat nursing her fingers in her lap, aware that all semblance of self-control had fled from her.

Antony played his move. 'Now use your knight to take his bishop,' instructed Tom. Harry moved the piece automatically, unable to concentrate on the game. Antony gave a whine

'I don't think I like playing with you,' he protested.

'You're too good.'

'That's the only way to improve your game,' said Tom calmly. 'You have to play with someone who's better than you. You'll get beaten time and time again, but you should never give up, because one day you'll beat them.'

Harry felt a flicker of annoyance. Oh, yes, he was very good at beating people down—people who couldn't stand up to him, like her and Antony. That was the kind of advice that only a man like him could offer. When had he ever been beaten at anything? she wondered. If he had, he'd know how dispiriting it was. He would have learned a little sensitivity. Her anger gave her confidence.

'But you're used to winning, aren't you?' she said aloud. And then, with a laugh that she hoped sounded flippant, 'Maybe you'd feel differently about it if you'd suffered a few defeats.'

Antony looked from one to the other, aware that all was not well between the two doctors. 'You flatter me when you assume I'm used to winning,' said Tom, and Harry was aware of the restraint in his voice. He moved another chess piece. 'Check.'

'It wasn't intended as flattery,' Harry replied. 'It was just an observation based on experience.' She hoped that Antony was too busy trying to salvage his position to take any notice of what they were saying. She glanced up to see what effect her words had had on the consultant. His eyes were narrowed and glittering. If she had been on her own with him she would have been frightened, but thank goodness Antony was there, like a buffer between them.

'Then your observation was inaccurate,' Tom said

bluntly. She was aware that he was looking round the ward, at the beds and the children in them. 'You obviously don't have enough experience to come to a useful conclusion. I've had my fair share of disappointment. Every day there's a new battle to fight. It still hurts every time I lose one.' He leaned past her and moved another piece on the chessboard. 'Checkmate.'

Harry felt as if she's been checkmated in their conversation, too. Just when she'd thought she'd found a way of getting at him, he'd dealt her a swift defeat. How clever he was. And how right he was to describe his work against cancer as a battle. He must have suffered many defeats on that particular battlefield. What an idiot she'd been not to have thought of that herself.

Antony, despite his defeat, was buoyant. 'You're good,' he beamed at Tom. 'Let's have another game. I want a chance to beat you. It's no fun playing with Harry. She's not good enough.'

'Antony,' she said sarcastically as she slid off the bedcover, 'your charm will get you everywhere. I'll leave you to the mercy of Dr Buchanan while I go and take some more blood from Pippa. And I hope he beats you again.'

'Well, try not to make Pippa scream as loudly as you did last time,' retorted Antony. 'I couldn't hear myself think.' Tom laughed, and with the sound of his amusement ringing humiliatingly in her ears Harry beat a retreat.

It was gone eight by the time Harry climbed wearily down the steps that led to her basement flat. She paused to check the soil in one of the big terracotta pots that flanked the door. It was bone dry. No wonder the daisies and lobelias were looking so droopy.

As she opened the door the noise hit her. Not the kind of noise that Paddington Ward produced, but the loud, insistent thump of pop music being played at full volume on the stereo. Hanging her bag on the old hallstand she'd salvaged from a junk stall in Portobello Road, she went into the sitting-room. It was a large room, low-ceilinged and painted entirely in white. She'd taken up the old carpet that had been down when she'd arrived, and spent three weeks of her spare time sanding and polishing the old floorboards, which now glowed with natural colour.

There wasn't much furniture in the room, for two good reasons. First of all, she didn't have enough money to fill the place with the things she liked. And secondly, Harry hated clutter. She'd grown up in a house full of knick-knacks and ornaments and bits of mismatched furniture, and this was the first chance she'd had to create her own environment. So there was just a big cream sofa, which she'd saved and saved for, a couple of low cream chairs which she'd bought second-hand and had covered, a simple pale wood coffee-table and an uncluttered shelving unit holding books, a small TV, and the stereo, which was still blasting away.

Harry strode over to the unit and turned the tape off. On the shelf next to it was a hand-thrown pottery bowl with a vivid abstract design painted on it. Someone had used it as an ashtray, and it was half-full of stubs and ash.

There was silence for a few seconds, as she surveyed

the room. The decoration was finished by three beautiful old kelim rugs that had been left to her by her grandfather, and the big mirror that sat on the mantelshelf and reflected the contents of the room. And then there were the plants. On each side of the french windows that led out to the small garden there were two lovely weeping figs, their leaves cascading in a green waterfall. Behind the sofa was a tall, impressive African hemp plant that she'd nurtured since it wasn't much more than a cutting. Outside on the patio were more tubs and pots filled with a variety of colourful plants that were just coming into brilliant flower.

Harry stood for a second, admiring them. It seemed a very middle-aged thing to admit, but she loved gardening and plants. When she'd had a hard day on the ward, there was nothing nicer than pottering in the garden for an hour or so, pulling out a few weeds here, transplanting something there. She looked out at the sky and wondered whether it would rain this evening. At that moment the bathroom door slammed.

'Why did you turn the music off? I was listening to it.' Gina came stomping into the room, one towel wrapped round her body and another round her head.

'I didn't think you were in,' Harry said mildly. 'At least, you weren't here.'

'I was listening to it in the bath, then you came in and turned it off.'

'Sorry.' Harry raised her hands in acknowledgement of her guilt. 'Did you have a good day at collegte?'

Gina looked evasive. 'Mmm,' she murmured, walking over to the stereo and switching it on again. She left a trail of water behind her on the polished floor.

'Turn it down, please,' asked Harry. Then suspiciously, 'You did go to college today?'

Gina turned to her. They shared the same slightly square face, the same grey-green eyes, the same generous mouth. Harry often thought, looking at her younger sister, that this was how she must look to other people. But then Gina would change her expression, or pull a face, and Harry was sometimes disturbed by what she saw. There was something devious about her these days. That was a terrible thing for a sister to say, but Harry had caught her out in so many little deceits. Gina gave her a wonderful, coy smile—the kind of smile intended to make the hardest of hearts melt.

'Actually, I didn't,' she admitted. 'I wasn't feeling well. My stomach was upset.'

'In that case you should have told me. I could have given you something for it,' replied Harry.

'I didn't realise until you'd gone—you left so early this morning.' Gina had turned away again, started to turn the music up. 'I'm mad, I'm bad . . .' she sang along with the Michael Jackson song.

Harry pressed the 'off' switch and suddenly it was just Gina singing the words. 'Look, you've got to go to college! It's the only way to get your typing and shorthand skills. Once you've got those you can do what you like.' She tried not to make it sound like nagging, but this had happened so many times in the last few weeks that she was beginning to lose her temper.

'That's all very well for you to say,' Gina pouted. 'You've never had to sit there and just type every day. It's the most boring thing in the world, and I don't want to do it.'

Harry gritted her teeth with exasperation. 'But it was

what *you* chose to do! I don't want to make a big issue of it, Gina, but it was you who went to the polytechnic and then dropped out after two terms. And it was you who decided to go on this course and learn typing, so that you could get a job.'

'Well, I've changed my mind.' Gina flounced back the way she had come, leaving more drips on the floor behind her. 'I'm not going back there.'

'What are you going to tell Mum and Dad when you go home, then?' Harry deliberately kept her voice down. Yelling didn't help anyone.

'That's something I need to talk to you about,' said Gina. And again there was that odd gleam in her eye. 'I thought I might stay here with you for a bit longer. The course was due to run for fifteen weeks. We're only seven weeks into it at the moment, so if I stayed here with you for the remaining eight Mum and Dad need never know. And after the eight weeks is up—well, I'd pay rent.'

'That's hardly the point. You haven't asked if I want to have you here permanently—and what will you tell Mum and Dad when you don't get the typing certificate and there's no job as a secretary?'

'I'll think of something.' Gina threw her another charming smile. 'I can't hang about arguing, Harry, I'm going to a party.' She paused, then offered, 'Why don't you come too? It would do you good to get out and meet people. You lead such a stuffy life. If you're not slaving away up at St Hugh's, you're just digging the garden, or something equally boring. You need to get out more. Why don't you let yourself go and have a good time, like me?'

'I could give you a hundred good reasons,' Harry said

flatly. 'But I won't because you'd find them just as boring and stuffy as everything else about my life.'

'If *that's* your attitude, there's nothing I can do about it.' Gina gave a shrug. 'Anyway, I'm going to enjoy myself, even if you aren't.' And with that she was gone, padding back to the bathroom.

Harry gritted her teeth. There was no point in arguing with her when she was in this kind of mood. Nothing you could say seemed to get through to her. She was a little, Harry reflected, like Tom Buchanan. Trying to argue with either of them was rather like hitting your head against a brick wall. They both knew exactly what they wanted; they both believed that they were right. And neither of them was prepared to give anyone else's views a chance.

Harry went and banged about in the kitchen, filling the watering can for the plants outside the front door. The kitchen was small and cosy, looking out over the white-painted basement area. There were simple pine units and a stripped pine table, all of which had been supplied when Harry had first moved in. She'd not made much attempt to decorate the place, but it was attractively full of things—utensils on shelves, spices and vinegar and oils sitting on the worktops and bunches of dried herbs hanging from hooks. Gina did not approve of it. She'd declared that it was a towny's version of a country kitchen. Harry had bitten her lip. Gina was eighteen and had a lot to learn—including doing the washing up after she'd cooked a meal, Harry thought, surveying all the dishes and pans piled in the sink.

As she watered the plants, she mulled over what had just been said. The idea of having Gina to stay for

longer than the original four months they'd agreed
appalled her. Maybe she had become too used to her
own company, but Gina had just swept in and taken
over. Harry had begun to feel a stranger in her own
home. It wasn't only the loud music or the fact that
Gina seemed to imagine there was an invisible servant in
the house who would pick up her clothes, cook her
meals and do her washing. She also undermined
everything Harry believed in. She declared that she
hated children and thought anyone who trained to be a
doctor was mad—years of slavery followed by years of
low-paid misery, that was how she'd summed up
Harry's career. She loved noise and bustle and bright
lights and hectic activity, all of which Harry could quite
happily live without. And then there were the young
men—Justin and Guy for the first couple of weeks and
since then someone called Paul. They'd taken to calling
in at all hours. They were all so silly and stupid—just
like Alex Buchanan, Harry thought grimly. And look
where that had got her.

'You're getting old, that's your problem,' she told
herself, coming back into the kitchen. But maybe it
wasn't just age. Perhaps she'd grown up the hard way.
Her brush with the Buchanans had certainly taught her
that life was a serious business.

She went to open the fridge. There were eggs, cheese,
smoked haddock, broccoli and salad things; she'd
bought them only a couple of days ago. Except that
there weren't. The fridge was practically bare. There
were a few spring onions, a tomato, a single egg and a
packet of frozen peas defrosting on the bottom shelf.
The freezer compartment, when she prized it open, was
completely filled by a huge tub of piña-colada-flavoured

ice-cream.

At that moment a car hooted outside the house. Harry couldn't see it, but she guessed it was someone who had come for Gina. There was a clatter of high heels on the hall floor. Harry raced out to catch her before she ran off. 'There doesn't seem to be anything left in the fridge,' she started, and then, 'Hey, is that my best skirt?'

'Oh, God! I'm sorry about the food. A couple of people came round at lunchtime and I made them smoked haddock with poached eggs and broccoli au gratin. It was very good.' Gina gave a sudden smile. 'Who knows, maybe I should take a cookery course! Don't worry, though,' she went on, seeing Harry's brow begin to darken. 'I'll get some more stuff tomorrow. Paul brought me some ice-cream, but I don't like it, so you can eat it all if you like. It's in the freezer.'

'Thanks a million,' Harry said glumly. 'And what about the skirt? What have you done to it? Why is it so short?' She stared aghast at her favourite skirt. It was gathered at the waist and made of swirly silk fabric covered in a muted pattern of soft apricot and green roses. It made her feel so feminine when she wore it with a silk blouse or her favourite cream linen jacket. Normally it fell to a couple of inches below her knees. But on Gina it was least five inches shorter. Harry bent to check it. 'You haven't . . .!' she exclaimed.

'I just shortened it,' protested Gina. 'It looks much better now I've cut the bottom off. No one wears longer skirts these days, and these flouncy ones are so pretty . . .'

'Do you have any idea how much that cost me?' Harry was pale with anger. 'You come here, you eat my food, ruin my clothes . . .'

'It's not ruined! You can still wear it. Your legs are good enough to get away with it,' Gina protested.

'That's not the point and you know it,' Harry continued, aware even as she said the words that they wouldn't make the slightest bit of difference. 'I'm not going to put up with it any longer.' There was more insistent hooting from outside.

'All right! Stop fussing. I'll pay you back,' muttered Gina rebelliously. 'I've got to go now, otherwise Paul will be furious.' And before Harry could stop her she had pulled open the front door and sprinted up the basement steps in a flurry of short skirt and stocking tops.

CHAPTER THREE

HARRY was deeply asleep when her bleeper, placed on the table beside her bed, went off. All the years of being woken in the middle of the night still hadn't accustomed her to that moment of confusion—the sense of not knowing where she was, or what she was doing there. Then, as always, she snapped into the routine response. She checked the time on the digital alarm: one fifty-five. On went the bedside lamp. Then she flung back the duvet, reached for the telephone and dialled.

'Dr Hart here. You bleeped me,' she told the switchboard operator, simultaneously reaching for the clothes she'd laid out before she went to bed. It was a habit all junior doctors developed and one which came in useful for the whole of their working lives. As the operator transferred her, she pulled on socks and stepped into her khaki-beige trousers.

'Sorry to call you out, Harry,' came the familiar voice of the A & E duty officer, 'but we've got a couple here who've brought in their baby. They think it's a fit, but we can't find anything wrong with him. They've asked to see a paediatrician.'

'Why isn't Steve Paige on duty?' Harry complained. 'He's supposed to be covering tonight.' She tucked the receiver under her chin and used both hands to fasten her trousers.

'He's in Theatre. We had a kid admitted with

abdominal pains earlier tonight and the consultant decided
to operate. Steve's tied up with that.'

'So you drag me out of bed instead,' moaned Harry,
with mock anger.

'You were doing something interesting, were you?' he
laughed.

'Unfortunately not. See you in about ten minutes.' It
took just two more minutes to slip into a cream polo-neck
sweater and a comfy pair of brown loafers, and to run a
brush quickly through her hair, which was loose. She
inspected herself in the mirror as she left the room. Maybe
she should have worn a bra with this sweater, but there
was no point in changing now.

It was strangely quiet in the street, but not far away she
could hear the traffic along the Bayswater Road. The car
was facing in the right direction. She chucked her bag on
the passenger seat, switched on the ignition and, lights
blazing, turned down Church Street and left at Kensington
High Street. There wasn't much traffic around and it was
easy to turn right into South Kensington. It always amazed
her that in the heart of such a busy, crowded city there
could be such an air of desertion at night.

She pulled into the staff car park precisely ten minutes
after she'd received the call. The Accident and Emergency
Department seemed pretty quiet and the duty officer was
waiting for her. 'It seems perfectly straightforward, but
the parents are insistent. Apparently the kid had been
crying for ages and suddenly stopped breathing for a few
seconds. It started again on its own and now it seems fine.'

Harry raised an eyebrow. 'OK. Where are they?'

He handed her the yellow case form, filled out with the
names and address and a brief description of the problem.
'They're in cubicle six.'

Harry scarcely needed telling. A tell-tale wail was emanating from behind the striped curtains of the sixth cubicle in the row. 'Hello, Mr and Mrs Atkinson,' she said, pulling back the curtain and walking in. 'I'm Dr Hart.'

'You're used to babies?' asked Mr Atkinson defensively. 'You're a paediatrician?'

'I specialise in children's medicine,' Harry assured him. Strictly speaking she wasn't entitled to call herself a paediatrician. That was a title only given to consultants.

'At last,' said the father. 'We've been waiting ages.' Harry ignored the remark, but took in the fact that he was extremely well-spoken and had draped a very expensive-looking leather jacket over the end of the examination couch.

'Now, what's the problem with you?' she asked gently, taking the baby from his mother's arms and rocking him slowly. 'You seem to be making enough noise now.' She turned to the parents. 'Does he always cry like this?'

'No, he's normally very quiet and good—which is one of the reasons we were so worried. He began to scream at teatime and kept going for hours. Then he fell asleep. I wasn't going to wake him up,' she explained, 'but he needed to be changed, and that set him off screaming again. And then——'

'My wife was just holding him, like you are now, when suddenly he stopped screaming. For a second he couldn't breathe. He just went stiff and he didn't move. He had a sort of glazed look. It was just like a fit.'

'And then?' prompted Harry, looking at the mother.

'Maybe seven or eight seconds later he sort of sighed

and started to breathe. He didn't cry at first, then he started again.'

Harry nodded and began to examine the child as she held him. He seemed sturdy and well formed. 'Do either of you have a family history of epilepsy?' she asked them. They both shook their heads. 'Shhh.' She rocked the baby and then, very gently, lowered her hand over his eyes to cut out the glare of the fluorescent lights. Gradually his sobs subsided.

'How did you do that?' asked the woman. 'I've been trying all evening to make him sleep.'

'It's just luck,' said Harry. Fairly early on in her training she'd discovered that she had the knack. There were some people who could pick up a happy child and immediately reduce it to howls of rage and unhappiness. And there were others, she among them, who seemed to have a calming presence on overwrought kids.

'He's four months, I see,' she said quietly, looking at the notes. 'Did you give him any medication when he couldn't sleep?'

'No, nothing,' said Mrs Atkinson firmly. 'I thought he might have indigestion so I gave him some gripe water——'

At that moment, right on cue, the child gave a massive burp. All three of them laughed. 'It looks as if you may have been right there,' smiled Harry. She touched the baby's forehead. Now he'd stopped crying he had begun to cool down. It was so difficult to tell with infants. They had no way of communicating what was wrong. When they got to a year, even to nine months or so, their behaviour was easier to interpret. But an infant like this would just scream and scream, regardless of whether its stomach or its ears hurt. That was a thought. She put the little chap down on the couch and used her torch to squint into his ears. No problem there. But when she put her hand on his tummy she found it was taut. She listened with her stethoscope. His stomach was churning away. Slowly she felt around his abdomen, watching his reaction for any sign of pain. There was none.

'I think,' she said carefully, 'he's got a stomach upset.'

'He had some fruit puree this morning,' interjected his mother. 'Now I come to think of it, I gave him something similar a few weeks ago and he was a bit crabby then.'

Harry felt the bits of the jigsaw coming together. 'Well, it looks to me as if that's it,' she said. 'Whatever it was you gave him may have upset him a bit. The evidence will come out in his nappies.'

'But what about this fit he had?' snapped the father, who had been brooding silently.

'I don't think it was a fit. I think it was more likely to be a breath-holding attack,' Harry said calmly. 'Fits tend to occur when a child has an infection. In this case I think what's happened is that your little boy's stomach has been hurting him, so he's been crying and crying. That's made him hot—so he's cried harder. You've probably noticed how when he cries he builds up a rhythm. Sometimes when a child is distressed this rhythm gets a bit confused. Instead of breathing in when they should, they breathe out. And, because they're in such a state, they can't catch their breath for a few seconds. They panic slightly and go stiff——'

'Oh, God!' said the mother. 'He might have died!'

'Oh, no,' Harry laughed. 'So long as there's nothing else wrong with him, the body automatically takes over. I think that's what happened with your son. The moment he lost control his brain automatically took over. A few seconds later he started to breathe normally again. If he'd had a proper fit I would have expected him to go floppy and black out.'

'I don't like the sound of this. Don't you think you ought to be doing some tests?' Mr Atkinson asked.

'Not tonight,' said Harry. 'We'll admit him for observation and see whether he feels better once whatever is troubling him is out of his system. Tomorrow we'll run a few checks to see whether he's suffering from an infection, or some kind of abdominal problem.'

'Something wrong with his stomach?' Mrs Atkinson looked even more alarmed than ever.

'Just a few routine tests to make sure that all he's suffering from is an upset stomach,' said Harry reassuringly. 'I'm certain that's all there is wrong with him, but we'll keep him here overnight just to be on the safe side. I'll just get the admission papers for you to fill out.'

'Why aren't you going to start doing something for him now?' Mr Atkinson asked bluntly. 'He might have another fit if you just leave him.'

Harry bit her tongue. How could she politely and tactfully make him understand that she'd met a dozen cases like this before? This was his only child—it was natural for him to be anxious. 'Because there's nothing that we *can* do right now. If you'd like me to go over what I told you, I'll be happy to do so——'

'I understood all that.' He cut her short. 'We'd like to see another doctor. A proper paediatrician this time.'

'John, please don't make a fuss. Dr Hart is going to admit him, surely that's enough?' Mrs Atkinson tried to intervene, but her husband was adamant.

'We have private health insurance, if that makes any

difference. But I promise you, we're not leaving here until our son has been seen by someone with more authority and something's done for him right now.' Harry clenched one hand in her trouser pocket, then reminded herself that getting angry was no way to deal with this kind of situation. She swallowed down her feelings, took a deep breath and was instantly calm.

'Very well. I'll try to find a registrar. I'm afraid you'll have to wait, and I don't know how long it will take.' As she emerged from the cubicle she bumped into the duty officer. 'Mr and Mrs Atkinson insist on seeing someone more senior—well, Mr Atkinson does, anyway.' She moderated her tone, aware that the couple were probably listening. 'You said there was an emergency admission. Is there anyone still around who could come and take a look?'

'Yes, you're in luck. He's here doing the admission paperwork.'

Harry walked back down to the broad counter which divided the waiting public from the staff. Her heart fell when she saw who it was standing there, filling in the forms that no one had had time to complete in the heat of the emergency. Tom Buchanan. She hesitated for a moment. He hadn't seen her. She could creep away and call up a registrar and he'd be none the wiser. She was just turning to go when he looked up.

'Hello, Harriet.' He smiled slightly. 'Busy night?'

She turned innocently back to him. 'I was called out to see the baby in cubicle six. It looks like a breath-holding attack and I want to admit him overnight, but the parents insist on a second opinion from someone with more experience.' She put in a cynical emphasis on the final word.

'Do you think I'll do?' he asked. His voice was deep and teasing; he was obviously amused by her behaviour. But though his gaze was quizzical, Harry couldn't help noticing how tired he looked. The hollows of his cheeks were emphasised by his three a.m. shadow. Then she realised that his eyes had dropped and he was looking at her with a new intensity. She remembered with horror that in her rush to come out she hadn't bothered with a bra, and she knew that he'd noticed it too. Not that she had anything to be ashamed of; it was just that she didn't normally flaunt herself, and she didn't want him to imagine that she made a habit of going bra-less—though why should she care what he thought?

'I'm sure you'll do very nicely,' she said witheringly.

The nurse who had come to call the next patient cast her a strange look. Housemen, even housemen from the paediatric unit, which was considered by many staff to be run on very lax lines, normally treated their consultants with the highest respect. And even if they didn't respect them, they were at least polite. 'Here are the notes,' Harry went on, handing over the clipboard. 'As I said, the Atkinsons are in cubicle six.'

Tom added his signature to the admission forms with a flourish, then took the Atkinson notes from her. 'You and I need to talk,' he said quietly, not looking at her.

Harry tried not to gulp. 'Mr and Mrs Atkinson can tell you everything you need to know. It's quite simple.'

'You know I don't mean that.' He stabbed the desk with his pen. 'Stop playing this stupid game with me.'

'I'm not playing any game,' she hissed, backing away.

'Then why,' he stepped towards her, 'did you try to avoid me just now? I saw you about to sneak away.' He reached out and took her by the wrist, and she felt his fingers burning her flesh like hot metal. 'We're going to have to learn to work together, whether you like it or not. That's why I want to talk to you.'

'The way you talked to me once before?'

'That's one of the things I want to discuss with you, but I can't seem to say more than a few words without you lashing out at me.'

Harry tried to draw away but he held her firmly. She knew he could feel how urgently the blood was pumping through her wrist. Her pulse was racing. 'I have *every* reason to lash out, as you well know.' She saw a flicker of something—embarrassment, perhaps—cross his face and it gave her courage. 'You'd better bear in mind that I know what you're really like, Dr Buchanan, even if everyone else around here thinks that the sun shines out of your ears. And now let me go,' she went on in a whisper, pulling her hand from his grasp. He released her, but his face was like thunder. 'Maybe some women like these caveman tactics, but I don't,' Harry concluded triumphantly. That had infuriated him, she could see, but before he could retaliate the duty officer rounded the corner and interrupted.

'Ah, you're still here, Dr Buchanan. The people in cubicle six are getting very impatient. I wonder if you could just take a look?'

'Yes, of course.' Tom straightened up. But he wasn't going to let her off that lightly. 'As I said before, Harriet, I think we need to discuss the situation.'

'I really don't think it's that important——' she stated, but he interrupted.

'Well, I do. We'll fix something tomorrow.' Harry had to bite her tongue. She couldn't protest, not with the duty officer watching.

'Very well, Dr Buchanan,' was all she could say. 'I'll go home now—if that's all right?'

He didn't even bother to reply as he walked off. The duty officer looked at her strangely. 'What's going on here, then?' he asked, amused. 'Do we have a lovers' tiff?'

'We certainly do not,' snapped Harry, and pausing only to grab her bag she set off for the car park. Unfortunately a quick getaway was out of the question. When she turned the key in the ignition nothing happened.

'Blast!' She tried again. Still nothing. Then she noticed that the headlight switch was pressed fully down. She'd left her lights on and drained the battery. It was the final straw. Gina, the Atkinsons, even Tom Buchanan—individually she could cope with them. But not all on the same night. She rested her face wearily in her hands, propped against the steering-wheel, and in bewilderment felt the dampness of tears on her cheeks. She was crying—tears of frustration and bitter disappointment. Tears that had been dammed up for as long as she could remember.

For the last few years she'd prided herself on keeping her life under strict control. A good, rewarding job, a nice flat, a few pleasant friends who didn't demand too much of her; it was all safe and unthreatening. Now two things in succession had come along to stir everything up—two things which she felt she really couldn't control. There was Gina, who seemed to take pleasure in reducing her to an exasperated heap, and Tom Buchanan, who in the space of less than twenty-four hours had demolished her to a snivelling wretch.

'Stop this,' she ordered herself aloud. 'Crying gets you nowhere. If either of them saw me now, they'd know they'd won again.' Resolutely she dried her eyes. She'd take a taxi home, she decided. There was little point in calling the AA now, it would take them too long to come. Locking the car, she made her way out of the hospital entrance and into the street. Almost as soon as she reached the pavement and began walking, a cab approached. Harry waved it down, but the driver didn't seem to see her and drove on. She muttered a rude word. Normally she didn't mind the twenty-minute walk home, but at this time of the morning the roads were unwelcoming. And, she realised with a shiver, the wind had got up. It was cold.

She'd turned into Kensington Gore and was heading for the High Street when she became aware that a car had begun to follow her. She heard the noise of the engine approaching behind her, but then it didn't overtake her as she'd expected. Whoever it was was just crawling along the kerb behind her. She gripped her case more firmly and took a look over her shoulder. It was a big black car. As she watched, it came right up to her side and stopped. The electric window began to come down with a little swish. Harry ran on ahead a few paces. If it was a kerb-crawler he'd get the message. But apparently he hadn't, because just a few seconds later he pulled up again, this time a few feet in front of her. Again she ran on past him, and this time she kept running until the bright lights of Kensington High Street came into view.

Running had made the blood pound in her ears and she didn't hear the noise of the engine until it was too late. This time the car drew up alongside and before she knew what was happening the driver's door had opened and a tall figure jumped out. She recognised him instantly, but she sprinted off all the same.

'Oh, no, you don't.' Tom Buchanan's long legs caught up with her easily and he grabbed her arm. She stopped short, and he almost cannoned into her. 'Harry——' he started, then paused with the realisation that as she'd tried to shake him off his palm had made firm contact with her breast, obviously unencumbered beneath her sweater.

Harry stifled a gasp, and turned her face away, trying to hide not just the fact that she'd been crying, but the blush his touch had brought to her cheek. A stabbing note of shock ran through her, but it wasn't entirely unpleasurable, she realised with horror. He let her go, then took her by the shoulders. For a moment she thought he was going to shake her like a child. She kept her head down, staring resolutely at the pavement like a misbehaving kid. If he was going to treat her like one, she'd act the part.

'What the hell are you playing at, walking around alone at this time of night?' he demanded.

'I'm going home—you gave me permission to do so,' she said coldly. Out of the corner of her eye she saw the familiar silhouette of a policeman, complete with helmet, coming towards them.

'Let me give you a lift. It's really not safe for you to walk about like this——'

Harry wrenched herself away. The policeman was almost upon them now, and it took only a few steps for her to walk defiantly up to him. This was madness, she thought to herself as she approached him. She didn't do things like this. She lived a rational, sane, well-organised life. What was happening to her?

'Are you all right, miss?' the policeman asked, seeing the car parked with its lights on and door open, and Tom standing passively by it, his hands thrust deep into his pockets.

'This man . . .' Harry started, and then paused. This

man, she wanted to say, was pestering her, being a nuisance, wouldn't leave her alone. But something held the words back. In her heart she wasn't proud of her behaviour; it wasn't like her to fight and antagonise others.

'What's the problem?' asked the policeman again.

'Yes, Harry, what's the problem?' echoed Tom, watching her closely. She'd been crying, he could see that now, and although he was furious with her he knew that it was his fault. He wasn't normally so inept at handling things. There was just something about her, something so defiant and pigheaded, that she made him lose his temper.

'You seem to be upset,' observed the policeman. 'Has something happened? Something you want to tell me about?'

'No, it's all right.' Harry held up her hands apologetically. 'Sorry, we were just having a disagreement and I . . .'

'We're colleagues up at the hospital.' Tom motioned in the direction of St Hugh's. 'Harry was walking home, and I was attempting to persuade her to let me give her a lift.'

The light of understanding began to dawn in the policeman's eyes. 'Oh, you're a nurse are you, miss? I see. Bit of a tiff, was it?'

'No, it was not,' snapped Harry, suddenly galvanised into life. 'I just want to walk home in peace. And I'm not a nurse.'

The policeman, whose manner had at first been all kindness, seemed taken aback by this display of irritability. 'Well if I were you, miss, and I had the offer of a ride home—from somebody I could trust, of course—I think I'd accept it. It's not a good idea to go walking around on your own at this time.'

Harry gritted her teeth. 'I *know*, I'm not walking home by choice. My car's in the hospital car park with a flat battery.'

'Then let me give you a lift.' Tom's voice was firm but soft. He was putting it on for the policeman's benefit, Harry thought darkly.

'It might make things easier,' said the policeman, obviously nervous that he was going to be left with an emotional woman on his hands. How, wondered Harry, was she going to get out of this one with her pride intact?

There was a long silence. She suddenly realised how very tired she felt. She had no fight left in her. 'All right,' she said flatly. 'You can drive me home. But I'm only accepting your offer because it seems the most practical alternative.'

Tom languidly opened the passenger door with a flourish and bowed as she got in. Harry steadfastly refused to look at him. She felt like a child who had behaved appallingly badly and knew it. All her natural instincts cried out to say sorry, but her pride prevented her from surrendering. She thought fleetingly how such a situation would end on Paddington Ward. The child would stubbornly refuse to give in and there would be a state of siege. Then she, or one of the other staff, would make a little peace offering—a smile, perhaps, or a treat. And suddenly there would be tears of remorse, a forgiving cuddle, and everything would be all right again.

Well, she thought to herself, there would be no friendly gesture from Tom Buchanan, and no surrender, no tears, and certainly no forgiving cuddle from her. Tom got in beside her and pressed the button that wound up the window. 'Are you all right?' he asked. With a start, Harry realised that there it was—that little conciliatory peace offering.

She said nothing, just reached for her seatbelt. It was stuck. She tugged but it wouldn't unreel. Tom silently leaned over and pulled. It gave way and he drew it across her. Momentarily his hand brushed her breast again and she felt her heart jolt. Was he doing it on purpose? she wondered angrily.

'I'll do that,' she said stiffly, taking it from him.

'Where do you live?'

Harry named the street and he put the car into gear and pulled smoothly out into the road. 'You were right about the Atkinson baby,' he said casually and Harry recognised the remark for what it was—another friendly gesture. But she couldn't be won over that easily. She was silent, aware, even as she sat there, that each moment she was getting deeper and deeper into trouble. Nothing was going to make her give in to him.

It took only a few minutes to reach her road. The houses in it were tall and elegant, with white and pale pink stucco fronts. He pulled up in the parking space vacated by her car. 'Thank you,' she said coolly, feeling for the door lock. It wouldn't open. She realised that the car probably had a central locking system that he could control. He switched off the ignition and turned to face her.

'Well, if I can't talk with you, I'll talk *at* you.'

Harry glared at him rebelliously. The urge to snap something at him was strong, but she resisted. The minute she started arguing with him, she would have compromised.

'You're the most infuriating woman I've ever met. Why are you behaving in such a childish way?' Exasperation was creeping into his voice.

'It's three in the morning,' she said with exaggerated

calm. 'I'm tired and I'm sure you are too. Please unlock the door and let me get out.'

He looked straight ahead for a second, thinking. Then he turned back to her. 'All right, if that's the way it's going to be.' He stared at her so hard she felt his eyes would bore through her. 'Report to my office at two tomorrow afternoon.'

'I've got a ward round with Phil Beech,' she said defiantly.

'Then I'll see you at six.'

'If nothing else comes up.'

His mouth was as hard as stone. 'Six p.m., Dr Hart. It's not a suggestion, it's an instruction. Now you can go.' He touched a switch on the dashboard and her door swung open.

'Very well, Dr Buchanan.' She got out, slammed the door, and without a backward look made her way down the basement steps. Behind her she heard him open his own door and watch, waiting until she was safely inside the flat before driving off.

'Damn him,' she muttered as she turned on the hall light. Tom Buchanan playing the part of the perfect gentleman was even more difficult to cope with than Tom Buchanan being his normal, overbearing, impossible self.

CHAPTER FOUR

HARRY peered through the narrow gap in the bedroom curtains. The sun was already shining and the local birds were into their post-dawn chorus songs. She looked at the clock again. It wasn't yet six, but she might as well get up. There was no point lying there worrying, which was exactly what she had been doing for the last few hours, since Tom Buchanan had dropped her off. Sleep was out of the question—a million thoughts raced through her mind and her heart thumped like an old engine. Maybe I should check my blood pressure, she mused as she went to wash and brush her teeth.

From the bottom drawer of the old pine chest of drawers she took her leotard and leggings and, discarding her nightdress, changed into them. There was one way of guaranteeing a good start to the day, Tom Buchanan or not, and that was to spend half an hour stretching and relaxing with some yoga exercises. She'd started yoga as a student, simply for the chance to get out once a week, rather than because she believed in it. But it worked. It really made her feel relaxed and able to face anything the world could fling at her. And although Jane Fonda wouldn't endorse it as strenuous exercise, Harry felt sure it helped keep her supple. She found a clip for her hair, then walked through to the living-room and put some Bach on the stereo, turning it down low so as not to wake Gina. And then, slowly, she started to bend and stretch, holding each position, closing her eyes and concentrating on her breathing, feeling her body at last begin to lose its tension and unwind.

By the time she'd finished, Harry felt much better. She'd even succeeded in putting thoughts of last night to the back of her mind—and that, she said to herself, was where they were going to stay. She took a quick shower and slipped into one of her more formal outfits, a full, sweeping navy skirt with tiny white dots. It came down to within a couple of inches of her ankles; there would be no comments about her knees today. She teamed it with a simple short-sleeved white silk blouse, and tied a delicate navy and white spotted shawl around her shoulders, knotting it at the front. An unobtrusive navy belt finished the outfit off—and very smart it looked too, Harry thought. She'd have to take the shawl off while she was working, and the blouse would probably get splattered with some nasty substance or other, but for her interview with Tom Buchanan she'd look thoroughly professional.

It had only just gone seven, and she was in the kitchen brewing coffee and eating a bowl of muesli, when she saw Gina trotting down the basement steps and fumbling for her front door keys. She had a smug smile on her face—a smile which disappeared as Harry let her in. 'Where have you been?' she asked. 'I thought you were in bed.'

'Don't start!' Gina threw up her hands. 'I've been out all night. And I know I didn't warn you, and I know what might have happened to me—but it didn't. I've had a wonderful time, and I'm quite old enough to take care of myself, thank you very much.' With a pout she stomped off to the boxroom which Harry had turned into a spare bedroom for her. As she went Harry noticed that her skirt, the pretty apricot one which Gina had shortened, was torn.

She went back to the kitchen, finished her coffee and muesli and swallowed with them all the angry things she wanted to say. When she'd washed up her mug and bowl, she walked calmly through to Gina's room. Her sister was lying in bed, mascara still streaked under her eyes, her clothes strewn all over the floor. As Harry came in Gina pulled the sheets up to her nose and pretended to be asleep.

'Don't be like this,' Harry said reasonably, picking up the skirt from where it had been hastily stuffed under the bed. 'I really don't mind you going out and enjoying yourself——'

'Hmmph,' came the reply.

'But you can't *just* have a good time. You've got to work a bit too, otherwise the fun gets boring.' Gina lifted her hand from beneath the sheet and gave a very long and loud impression of a yawn.

'I know it's very boring of me to say so. But it's also very dangerous for you to go off with strange young men for the whole night. Where did you go?' Harry asked, feeling increasingly like some kind of interrogator, yet knowing it had to be said for Gina's own good.

'It's none of your business.' Gina turned over and presented her back to Harry.

'Of course it's my business!' Harry winced. She was beginning to sound like some nagging, disapproving old killjoy. 'This is London and there are a lot of strange people about. You have to be careful. Can you imagine how I would have felt if something terrible had happened to you and I didn't even know you weren't tucked up safely in bed?'

'I expect you'd have been pleased,' Gina responded. 'You don't like me. You moan at me all the time——'

'Oh!' The calming effect of the yoga was short-lived. Harry thumped her sister through the duvet—not a hard blow, but enough to express her exasperation. 'Why do you always have to play these stupid games with me?' She stopped short for a moment, hearing Tom Buchanan's voice echoing in her ears. She blotted it out quickly. 'I care about you, that's why, and I can't think of anything worse than you getting into trouble.'

'So you'd like me to get my typing certificate and then go home and live with Mummy and Daddy and be a little goody-goody, just like you were,' came the whine from under the covers. 'Well, I'm not going to. I'm going to enjoy myself and I don't care whether you like it or not.'

'Give me strength,' muttered Harry. 'You're just manipulating everything I say.' There was silence from under the bedclothes. 'In future,' Harry continued, 'as a matter of courtesy to me as your landlady, I'd like to know where you're going each evening. Not just whether you're going to a party or out for a meal, but the address, who you're going with and what time you intend to be back.'

'No!' Gina shot upright in bed, her cheeks blazing. 'You have no right to check up on me like this. I'm not a child.'

'Then stop behaving like one. When I get back from work tonight I want to see a note on the kitchen table telling me where you've gone and where I can contact you.'

'You sound just like Mum! You've got no right to dictate my life like this.' Gina's eyes were filling with tears—whether of rage or because she was genuinely upset, Harry wasn't sure.

'You came to stay here while you studied.' She tried to sound cool and unflustered, which was difficult. 'That was fine by me, but you've now given that up. You can either behave and stay, or you can pack your bag and go home, because you're not using my flat like a hotel. And there's another thing, Gina. If you want to be treated like an adult you'll have to behave like one. That includes doing your own washing-up, cleaning your own room and doing your own food shopping. If you keep on behaving like a child, I'll just have to treat you like one.' Harry gritted her teeth; once more she heard the faint echo of Tom Buchanan's words to *her*.

'Go away and leave me alone,' muttered Gina.

'OK.' Harry went to the door. 'But when I get back from work I want to see the kitchen clean and tidy, the bathroom gleaming, and plenty of decent food in the fridge. You can eat junk food if you want, but I'd like something that doesn't come out of a packet.' As she shut the door behind her, Harry heard a thump as Gina threw something. She turned and opened it again. 'And by the way, we need loo paper, so put it on your shopping list.' Before the second shoe came flying, she'd slammed the door shut again.

Well, she thought, as she set off for the hospital, she hadn't handled *that* very well. Now it looked as if it was war on all fronts.

Harry was going through the morning's test results in the office she shared with Steve Paige when he arrived unexpectedly. 'I thought this was your day off?' she asked.

Steve inched into the cramped space carrying his sports bag in one hand and his briefcase in the other. 'I wanted to come in and see how last night's emergency admission is doing,' he confessed, looking around for enough room to dump his bag. He eventually managed to balance it on the top of a filing cabinet.

'Give me the details,' Harry asked absent-mindedly. 'Oh, that's good.' She waved a test report at him. 'Maria Margolyes' jejunal biopsy results are back and they're practically screaming coeliac disease. We'll have her on a gluten-free diet by lunchtime.'

Steve nodded. 'That's good—another mystery solved. While I'm here I ought to tell you about this girl who came in last night. You'll no doubt be dealing with her today. When she came in we diagnosed her as having appendicitis and possible peritonitis.'

'I know, I heard,' said Harry. 'Why did Buchanan get involved with it? Surely the surgical team could have been trusted to deal with a ruptured appendix by themselves?'

'It turned out not to be that simple. The X-rays showed a mass in her abdomen and when we opened her up we found a neuroblastoma——'

'A malignant tumour,' Harry said almost to herself.

'Exactly, so it was decided to call Buchanan in to deal with it. He is, after all, our new cancer specialist,' added Steve. 'He removed it. He seems very good. He spent a long time talking to the parents.'

Harry was thinking. When she'd seen him in A & E last night she hadn't stopped to ask herself what he was doing there. She'd just assumed—well, she didn't know what she'd assumed. Perhaps she would have treated him a little differently if she'd known he was just out of Theatre. She shook herself. That was no way to start thinking!

'How was she? Have you seen her this morning?'

'Yes, she's very weak. We'll have to get her back on her feet before starting chemotherapy—poor kid. Her name's Patsy Cox and she's a little sweetheart, so keep an eye on her for me, will you?'

'Of course I will.' Harry got up to go.

'After what you told me about Buchanan I expected him to be a monster.' Steve lounged in his chair. 'But he seems OK. Quite human, in fact. He was good with the parents last night.'

'I never said he wasn't a good doctor.'

'You never said that he was tall, dark and handsome, either.' He gave her an accusing look. 'The nurses in A & E and Theatre were very taken with him.'

'Really?' Harry tried to be dismissive. 'He's not the type to interest me. Anyway, he's probably got a wife and four kids.'

Steve shook his head. 'Oh, no, he hasn't. Sister on A & E asked him outright—what a bold hussy she is,' he added in a silly voice. 'You should have seen the look on her face when he told her that he was unattached—sheer ambition, that's what it was. Why don't nurses feel that way about me?'

'Because most of them are taller than you?' Harry suggested. Steve was just under five and a half feet high, and it was a standing joke that he'd chosen to go into paediatrics because it was the only area of medicine where he was guaranteed to be taller than his patients.

'That's below the belt,' he complained, rummaging through his drawer. 'In view of your last remark I think I should tell you that according to the duty officer in A & E there's something going on between you and Buchanan.'

'What?' Harry stopped abruptly.

'Rumour has it that you and Dr Buchanan were interrupted in the middle of a ding-dong argument in A & E last night. I should think Sister will be after your blood.'

'It was scarcely an argument,' Harry said firmly, 'it was just . . .'

'It was an argument.' Steve grinned. 'Have you ever heard a houseman argue with a consultant before now?' Harry was silenced. Housemen did what consultants told them—if they valued their jobs, that was. 'I'm just repeating what I've heard. According to the hospital grapevine, there's something cooking between you two.'

'That is absolutely ridiculous!' stormed Harry. 'I hate——' She paused and tried to put it into perspective. 'I dislike the man intensely, and you can tell Sister A & E that on my behalf. She's welcome to him.'

'Well, there's no smoke without fire,' replied Steve, his eyes dancing with delight at the storm he'd blown up. 'And from what I've heard, you and Buchanan had quite a bonfire burning.'

'Well I'm going to pour a bucket of water on it right now,' Harry responded coldly.

'Just thought you might like to know, that's all.' Steve waved his hands in a show of innocence. 'You can't blame me, but maybe you should keep things a little more tightly under control, Harry. It's not like you to stand around arguing with senior clinicians in public places. Everyone knows that, and they're trying to find a reason for your sudden change in behaviour.'

'It's his fault—he started it first.'

'Harry, even the kids on Paddington know that isn't a good enough excuse! Whatever's in the past, forget it. He seems to be a reasonable kind of bloke. Maybe he's changed since your last encounter! You're never going to win a fight with him, so why not try some quiet co-existence?'

Harry attempted a curtsy, but there wasn't sufficient room in the office for her to pull it off. 'Thank you so much for your concern,' she said with heavy irony. 'If you ever decide to give up medicine you could have a great career as an agony aunt. Now I've got to go. See you tomorrow.'

'Before you go, are you free to come to a party on Saturday evening? I know it's a bit last-minute, but one of my flatmates is going to Chicago and we thought we'd have a party to send him off.'

'Thanks, but . . .' Harry looked at him dubiously. 'I don't really know any of your friends——'

'Half the staff here are already coming. Pat O'Brien's said yes, so there's no need to worry about not knowing anyone. It'll be fun to see each other outside this boring old building. How about it?'

Harry smiled. Parties weren't really her cup of tea—she hated standing in corners yelling at strangers above the music—but she didn't want to tell Steve that. 'All right, thanks,' she nodded. 'It sounds like fun.' And, she thought to herself, he'd probably never notice if she didn't turn up on the night.

It was an operation day down on Paddington, and Harry was kept busy checking children on their way to and from Theatre and reassuring their anxious parents. Then around midday there was a slight emergency when three small children were admitted for a stomach wash after they'd eaten their way through a packet of pills they'd found in a handbag. Harry, aware that the clock was ticking away, found herself explaining the procedure not to just one mother, but three, and to make matters worse, the mother who had been minding the children was in floods of hysterical tears.

'There's no point in blaming yourself,' Harry comforted her, having heard how the accident happened. 'Sometimes these things happen, despite all your precautions. We caught the children in time and there's no harm done, so please, stop these recriminations. Just go and give your daughter a good cuddle.'

By the time she was free to get around to the more routine tasks, it was getting ominously close to four o'clock, and well after five before she got round to carrying out a lumbar puncture on young Patrick Millstead.

'Ow,' he moaned, trying to wriggle out of the nurse's grasp.

'Sorry,' said Harry, genuinely grieved at the discomfort she was causing him. 'Not long now, Patrick, we're doing well. What's number one in the pop charts this week?' she asked, trying to distract him.

'Don't you know?' he asked disbelievingly.

'Not this week. Do *you* know?'

'Michael Jackson—of course,' he added with contempt.

'I should have known. It was bound to be Michael Jackson,' Harry mused. With one gloved hand she inserted the tap on to the end of the needle that she had inserted into his spine. The nurse at her side held out a sterile container and Harry gently jiggled the needle until the fluid began to flow. 'Is it clear?' she asked the nurse, who held it up to the light for her inspection. 'Bingo! The worst is over, Patrick. Keep still for just another minute. We need one more sample.' Using the tap, she filled another container with the cerebrospinal fluid that contained important clues in diagnosing his illness.

It was the work of another two minutes to withdraw the needle and swab the area clean. 'What colour sticking plaster would you like?' she asked her patient, who was being held in a firm wrestling lock by the staff nurse.

'Red,' came his half-smothered reply. 'A really big one.'

'You can have the biggest red one we've got,' laughed

Harry, applying it over the puncture mark. 'There, it's all over. Good lad.'

The staff nurse released him from his curled position. He rubbed himself and announced, in his heavy *East Enders* accent, 'That was bloody awful.'

'Language, Patrick,' the nurse said, hiding her smile.

'Well, it was,' he moaned. 'Don't I even get a sweet?'

'Of course you do. There's one in your ear, look.' As she turned towards him Harry deftly removed a sweet from her pocket and pretended to magic it from his ear. He was unimpressed.

'It's not real magic like they have on the telly,' he complained. 'Why can't you make that Prakesh kid disappear? He's a bloo——'

'Patrick,' warned the nurse.

'He's a flaming nuisance,' he finished. 'He does nothing but cry all the time.'

'With a bit of luck he'll be going home soon,' said Harry. 'That's the only way I can make my patients disappear. I want you to stay in bed for the next two hours, please. If we put the little TV at the end of your bed you can watch it.'

'I've missed all the kids' programmes. It's just the six o'clock news,' he complained.

'Sorry about that,' said Harry. 'You watch the news, and if you get a headache or your toes go tingly, let one of the nurses know, won't you?'

'OK,' he said wearily, sounding at least fifty years older than his real age. 'I get the message.'

Pat O'Brien stuck her head around the treatment room door. 'Before you go, can you have a look at Patsy Cox? Her last painkiller's wearing off and she's uncomfortable.' Harry glanced again at her watch. Well, even Tom

Buchanan would agree that duty came first. There was nothing for it, he was going to have to wait for her.

It was gone six-thirty when she walked calmly down the corridor to the consultants' offices. Maybe, she thought wickedly, he'd gone home in disgust and she could avoid the confrontation that she knew was coming. She knocked quietly at his door, with its shiny new sign displaying his name.

'Come in.' Taking a deep breath, she entered. He was sitting at the desk writing something, and it took a few moments before he looked up at her. 'Sit down.' He motioned towards the chair opposite the desk. Harry registered the fact that today he was dressed in sober dark grey, with a white shirt—and the most amazing tie she'd seen. It was hand-painted silk, she guessed, having seen something similar in expensive shop windows, and it was decorated with a jazzy, but not dazzling, abstract design in greens and sea-blues that reflected the colour of his eyes. He noticed where her eyes were straying.

'I like it,' he said simply, putting down his pen, 'even if it has raised a few eyebrows among my fellow consultants.'

'I like it too,' said Harry without thinking, and then wondered why she was volunteering an opinion.

'Good. At least we agree on one thing.' He got up and walked round to her side of the desk, then perched on it, his legs almost brushing hers—much too close for comfort. Again Harry was struck by the overwhelming maleness of him. In all her experience, both personal and medical, she'd never known a man who exuded such masculine energy—such uninhibited virility. He must, she thought, be positively sizzling with male hormones. Perhaps that explained why she felt so threatened when he

was near—some primeval female survival instinct warning
her to keep away from this explosive, unpredictable,
overpowering male.

'Sorry I'm late,' she said defensively, shaken by her
thoughts. 'I was busy with Patsy Cox. She was
uncomfortable so I gave her a top-up shot of morphine
sulphate.'

'I know. I called Pat O'Brien to find out if you were
there.' He paused, recognising the flash of indignation
that lit her eyes. 'Forgive me,' he added with heavy irony,
'but I suspected that you might simply try to slip away
without seeing me. You're not going to tell me that the
thought didn't cross your mind?'

Harry didn't deny it, but she couldn't resist a few words
of protest. 'I don't like being checked up on.'

'If you started behaving like a reasonable adult I
wouldn't feel the need to do it,' he shot back instantly.
'And that's why we're here this evening. You know as well
as I do that you can't allow your personal animosity to
spill over on the ward.'

'*Our* personal animosity——'

'No, *yours*. I've got nothing against you.' He leaned
closer. 'Ever since you saw me you've been hostile,
impossibly difficult to deal with. I'm too deeply
involved with my work to sustain this feud—and you
know as well as I do that any bad feeling between us gets
transmitted to the patients. It's going to have to stop.'

She tilted her chin defiantly and maintained a dignified
silence. 'You're doing it again now,' he said accusingly.
'How can I forge a working relationship with you when
you won't even talk to me?'

'You know damn well what's wrong. Don't tell me
you've forgotten our first meeting?'

'No,' he said more thoughtfully, 'I haven't, but that's in the past. I'm very sorry about it, and I wish that things hadn't happened as they did.'

'I suppose that's as near to an apology as I'm going to get,' Harry responded curtly. 'Let's just forget it, is that it?'

'Why not? For pity's sake, it was six years ago! Most people would have reduced it to an insignificant incident, but you've kept your resentment against me boiling all this time.' He eyed her keenly. 'What's wrong, Harry? Why are you still shouldering this massive grudge?'

She sat silently brooding. Here he was, doing it all over again, dominating and imposing his view of things. Whatever she thought or felt didn't count as far as he was concerned. 'This is just like last time,' she said hollowly, voicing her thoughts. 'You come steaming uninvited into my life and impose your interpretation of events on me. First, Alex had that car crash and you succeeded in laying all the blame at my door. And now, because I'm not worshipping the ground you work on, like most of the other staff around here, who don't know what you're really like,' she threw in snidely, 'you're telling me that *I've* got a problem.'

Triumphantly, she watched him wince. One or two of her verbal blows were hitting home, and the knowledge gave her courage and fire. 'Well, Dr Buchanan,' she hit out again, 'the problem is all yours, because this time I'm not the naïve, impressionable little medical student you once steamrollered so thoroughly. I'm not simply going to do everything you say——'

'Then you're going to find life on Paddington Ward very difficult,' he interrupted curtly, 'because you're going to be my houseman.'

'What?' Harry looked at him, disbelieving what she'd just heard.

'You're going to work on my firm.'

'Not if I have any say in the matter.'

'You don't. Phil Beech and I discussed it this morning. Now there are two consultants as well as two registrars and two housemen, it seems logical to divide into two independent firms. Naturally we'll all have to be prepared to cover for each other, but you'll get a chance to concentrate more on my patients.'

'What if I don't want to?' Harry tried to keep her voice steeled against him, but despite her efforts she felt herself wavering in alarm.

Tom turned to look out of the window, to the grimy rooftops of the hospital. His strong, lean physique was silhouetted against the light. Harry felt another betraying surge of appreciation of his sheer animal magnetism.

'Phil felt pretty certain it would suit you. He says you're very good with the seriously ill children and that parents have confidence in you. That's important when you have a child who may be here for months, with the parents practically living here too. You know what paediatrics is like—it's about families, not just individual patients.' He turned back to face her with a knowing smile. 'Besides, Phil said that as soon as you heard about the unit you read every book on childhood cancer you could lay your hands on.'

Harry bit her lip, dismayed. She had come to expect criticism from this man, not compliments. 'And has anyone bothered to ask Steve Paige if he's interested in joining your firm?'

'I had a word with him last night and he confirmed what Phil had told me. He's more interested in infants and neonates than older children.'

'You seem to be presenting me with a *fait accompli*.' Harry felt as if she was drowning in confusion. He was handing her the job she'd wanted on a plate, and she could do nothing but complain. If only he'd been an ugly, balding little man with bad breath and thick glasses everything would have been perfect. But he wasn't. He was the most virile, striking man she had ever met, and he seemed capable of doing nothing but undermining her at every turn.

'I suppose so,' he agreed. 'But if it suits you, why kick against it?'

Because of you, Harry wanted to say, but the words wouldn't come out.

'You realise that I could make your life in this hospital very difficult? I won't hesitate in causing a fuss if your attitude affects the patients on Paddington Ward.'

'My attitude towards the patients is fine, no one's ever questioned that. As for my attitude towards you . . .' She paused, wondering how far she dared to go. 'It hasn't changed one iota.' A lump rose inexplicably in her throat and she had to swallow.

Before she knew what was happening he'd reached out and grabbed her by the shoulders. She recoiled and he shook her, his fingers biting into her flesh. 'You're heading for trouble, Harry.' His hands relaxed their grip slightly, but he still pinned her into the chair, his legs rubbing against hers, his face just a few inches from her own. 'You're forcing me to make threats, and that's the last thing I want to do. If we can work together, if you'll co-operate with me for just a week or two, you'll see I'm not the unreasonable ogre you believe me to be. You've got to get this chip off your shoulder, otherwise you'll be committing professional suicide. You can't hold me responsible for that.'

Harry forced herself to remain calm, despite the welter of fury and alarm, and some half-defined longing, that clashed in her stomach. 'I'll hold you responsible for everything,' she said flatly, but also strangely exhilarated, by the thunder in his face. She restrained the desire to touch him, but her fingers itched to feel the smooth, tanned skin of his cheek and the roughness of his hair. In the burning, clear blue of his eyes she sensed a reciprocal desire. What might have happened she didn't know, but at that moment the telephone rang. Silently he let her go and walked round the desk to pick up the receiver, his eyes blistering her all the while. From the brief conversation Harry sensed that there was a medical crisis.

'I'll be there as soon as possible,' he promised, then rang off. 'You've been saved by the bell,' he said tightly, reaching for his briefcase and throwing his belongings into it. 'I have to go over to Highstead to see one of my old patients.'

'Saved from what?' Harry blurted, suddenly brave now he was on the other side of the desk and had his back turned to her. 'More threats and violence? Or a fate worse than death, perhaps?'

He sprang round and she saw the flush of anger across his cheekbones. 'I think that's more likely to be wishful thinking on your part.'

Harry tried to breathe and found she couldn't. It seemed as if she sat there as the minutes ticked by, fighting for air. At last her lungs stopped gasping and her heart began to pound like a drum against her ribs. 'How dare you?'

He didn't answer, but the look he cast her as he swept

out was full of contempt. And why should it be any different? Harry thought, rising unsteadily to her feet. He'd never shown her anything but contempt—contempt for her feelings, her thoughts, the truth—and nothing was going to make him change.

CHAPTER FIVE

'I DON'T believe it!' Harry stood in the sitting-room of her flat, her briefcase still in her hand, and surveyed the scene before her. She'd walked into the hall and almost tripped over the first of a long, meandering line of loo rolls which led, like a rainbow-coloured trail, into the sitting-room, where it disappeared under the coffee-table and round the back of the sofa. She followed it out of the sitting-room and into the corridor at the back of the flat, where the bathroom and her bedroom were situated. The very last loo roll, a pink one, was positioned in the middle of the bathroom floor and to it was pinned a note.

'Well,' Gina had written, 'you did tell me to buy more loo rolls. Hope you're impressed. Don't get furious about the money because they're a gift from Paul. We've gone out to dinner and a party. Back very late—or very early. Don't worry!'

Harry crumpled the paper in her fingers and sat on the edge of the bath. What a sight! She allowed herself a brief giggle at the joke before forcing herself back to sober reality. How many of the damn things were there? She followed the trail back into the sitting-room, trying to collect them up and count them at the same time. Fifty-six in all, she made it. A whole year's supply! And what must it all have cost? More to the point, where on earth was she going to keep them?

Before she could work out the answer, the doorbell rang. 'Thank goodness you're in!' Anthea Robson, who lived in the house upstairs, practically fell in the door. 'Panic stations, Harry,' she gasped breathlessly. 'I've got to go to Heathrow. Would you be an angel and keep an eye on Melanie for me?'

Harry was unperturbed. Anthea lived in a state of almost permanent panic. 'Of course I will. How long are you going to be?' Harry put down the armful of toilet rolls she'd been cradling. 'Do you need me right now?' She could feel her stomach working itself up to a growl of hunger.

'I'm afraid I do—it's an emergency, as usual.' Anthea peered at the multi-coloured stack on the hall floor. 'Very interesting. Have you taken up modern sculpture? What an amusing idea.' Anthea taught art at one of the major London art colleges and was always on the lookout for new trends.

'No!' Harry grinned. 'I told Gina we needed some more and this is her idea of a joke. Fifty-six rolls of it. If you ever run out, you know where to come.'

'You could always try persuading the Tate Gallery to give you a fortune for them,' mused Anthea, fumbling for the keys to her car. 'It'll only take me an hour or so. Thanks a million, Harry. I don't know how we'd survive without you.'

'Flattery'll get you everywhere.' Harry waved her off, then let herself into the main part of the house. The hall was long and elegant, with plaster mouldings around the high ceiling and above the doors. The walls were hung with Anthea's paintings and blown-up black and white pictures taken by Terry, her husband, who was a professional photographer. 'Where are you, Melanie?'

Harry called.

'In here.' Harry walked down towards the kitchen at the back of the house, overlooking the garden. It was a long, bright room with a stripped board floor and oak units. There were more paintings everywhere, some propped on the floor waiting to be found a space. Melanie sat at the table drawing. She looked up as Harry came in. 'Hi!' And with a fluid movement, born of long practice, she manoeuvred her wheelchair away from the table.

As usual, Harry experienced a split second of shock at seeing the chair. She didn't really understand it; after all, she knew better than anyone that Melanie was never going to get out of it and walk. But she was such a pretty child and the wheelchair was so cumbersome. Harry kissed her on the cheek. 'There's no need for you to come in and look after me, you know. I'm quite capable of looking after myself for a few hours,' she chided. 'Mum's so disorganised, and then she gets in a flap and won't leave me on my own. Dad bought her a Filofax for Christmas but she can never remember where she put it.'

Harry laughed. 'You're wicked! Where's your Dad at the moment? Somewhere exotic?'

Melanie stuck out her tongue in dismissal. 'No, only Hong Kong. But he's back from there tonight. Mum's gone to meet him from the airport—only she nearly forgot.'

'It's all right for some! I wouldn't mind going to Hong Kong.'

'I went last year, and it was boring,' Melanie complained. 'Too many people everywhere. Nearly as boring as when we go to the house in Tuscany. I'd rather go back to Disneyland again.'

'You globetrotters—you don't know what real life's like,' sighed Harry ruefully. Despite her disability, Melanie had seen more of the world and led a more interesting life than most children her age. 'I haven't seen you for more than a week. What exciting things have you been up to?'

Melanie chattered as she copied a picture of a pop star from a magazine. It was very good, Harry reckoned, even if the pop star himself was little more than a pimply blond youth. Melanie had obviously inherited her mother's artistic talent. Why did girls go crazy over such bland looks? Now, if he'd been dark, with sea-blue eyes . . . She stopped herself short, the image of Tom Buchanan's face imprinted on the blank sheet of paper in front of her. There was no denying he was good-looking. She wasn't such a fool as to pretend that he wasn't. She shut her eyes for a second and willed the picture of him to vanish, but the blue eyes wouldn't disappear. They seemed to be watching her from inside her own head, raiding her thoughts, haunting everything she did.

'We went to London Zoo on Sunday. Have you been there?' asked Melanie.

'Not recently,' Harry admitted.

'It's so sad. All those poor animals in cages, unable to run around and enjoy themselves. I suppose it's a bit like being stuck in a chair when everyone else can walk. I didn't like it very much.' Melanie frowned. 'Do you want to play Trivial Pursuit?'

Harry nodded. Anything to take her mind off Tom Buchanan. Melanie went to fetch the big blue box that held the junior version of the game. The wheels of the chair squeaked on the wooden floor as she propelled herself into the other room.

'Hey, come here!' she called. 'I forgot. Mum finished the picture. Come and see.'

Harry followed her into the sitting-room. There were more paintings everywhere, including one propped up on a chair. 'What do you think? asked Melanie.

Harry looked and saw herself. Anthea had caught the mood of the moment perfectly. She'd been nagging Harry to sit for her for ages, and one Sunday morning she'd dragged her up to the studio on the top floor and positioned her on a stool at a table. Harry could remember how tired she'd been; it had been a long, hard week on Paddington Ward. She'd leaned her elbows on the table, rested her chin on her hands and cast Anthea an expression that contained both amusement and resignation. And that was exactly what the picture showed—a calm, resigned exterior, the tired shadows under her eyes and, deep within them, a glint of cool green defiance. It was a flattering picture, which she hadn't expected because Anthea wasn't interested in painting portraits for people who wanted the size of their nose diminished or their freckles banished. Even so, there was something in the face, something distant and defensive, which bothered Harry as she surveyed it.

'Is it really me?'

'Oh, yes, it's good. Mum was pleased. She said she'd got your wariness.'

'Me, wary?' Harry was startled. Melanie went pink.

'Sorry, I don't think she meant it to sound nasty. It's just that sometimes you look . . .' Harry waited. Melanie looked up at her, obviously weighing her words carefully. 'I know what Mum means. Sometimes you look as if you're trying to keep the world at arm's length. It's probably just because people keep asking you to do them favours,' she added thoughtfully. 'Mum said you can have the picture if you want it, but she wants to exhibit it first.'

Harry shuddered. No, she didn't want it. It was too revealing. She wasn't sure she was happy about being the woman on the canvas. 'It's kind of her, but I'm not sure I could live with myself,' she said, trying to make it sound jokey. 'Come on, let's go back into the kitchen and play Trivial Pursuit.'

They set out the board and the pieces and began to play, throwing the dice and asking each other questions.

'What's the name of Dennis the Menace's dog? Easy!' cried Melanie.

'Gnasher,' said Harry smugly.

'How do you know that?'

'I read *The Beano* most weeks. We doctors have to keep abreast of all the latest publications,' Harry teased. 'What's that?' There was a distant ringing sound.

'That's your doorbell. When it's quiet—when no one's playing records really loud,' Melanie added darkly, 'we can hear it.'

The point was not lost on Harry. She would have to insist that Gina kept the noise down in future. 'I'd better go and see who it is. Don't cheat while I'm away.' She sprinted down the hall, opened the door and leaned over the railings. 'Hello?'

'Hello.' Tom Buchanan's dark head tilted upwards. Harry felt a flash of anger that he should have invaded her territory without an invitation, but it was quickly superseded by the sensation of invisible icy fingers tracing a pattern up and down her spine. 'I thought you lived down here?' he asked.

'I do,' Harry said coolly. He waited for an explanation but she didn't offer one.

'Can I come up and see you? Or maybe you could come down?'

'I'm busy.' He began to climb the basement steps towards her. 'I won't be a minute, Melanie,' she called.

'Busy all evening?' he asked, when he got to the pavement level.

'Yes.' Harry heard the thrumming of Melanie's wheelchair approaching down the hall. Her heart began to race. Whatever happened, he mustn't see Melanie. 'I'm child-minding, so I'd better go.' She turned to go inside and shut the door on him, but he reached out and took her arm.

'Hold on. We have unfinished business.' He was looking at her too closely, and his voice was ominously quiet and calm. The calm before the storm. Where he touched her, sheets of burning sensation began to pulse under the skin.

Melanie's youthful voice interrupted them. 'I heard what you said, Harry. I'm not a child,' she complained. 'Who is it?'

'Just somebody from the hospital,' Harry said, trying to usher her back inside. 'Let's go back in.' But Melanie pushed forward, the chair striking hard on the backs of Harry's legs.

She risked a sweeping glance at Tom's face and registered the blank surprise as he absorbed the scene. He opened his mouth to say something, then thought better of it. Harry watched the impact wash over him; the aggression so obviously lurking beneath the surface had subsided, to be replaced by shock. He looked suddenly tired, as if unhappy memories had been revived. His hand dropped from her arm. Melanie's voice again broke the silence.

'What is it? An emergency? You can go if you need to, I'm quite all right on my own. Mum would understand.'

'No, it's not an emergency,' Harry said quietly. Tom tore his eyes away from the wheelchair.

'So you're busy all evening?' His voice was dry and throaty—the sound made by a man who had just seen a ghost.

'Yes,' said Harry firmly.

'No,' contradicted Melanie at precisely the same second. 'My Mum and Dad will be back before long.'

Tom was still staring at her as if he couldn't accept the evidence of his eyes. Harry wondered what he was thinking. Like most doctors, he was good at hiding his feelings; it was something you learned early in your medical career. There was no point in alarming patients and their relatives by revealing your own worries and fears. 'If you're not going to be long, I'll sit in the car and wait for you,' he suggested. 'We have things to discuss.'

'There's *nothing* to discuss, not after this afternoon. You made yourself perfectly clear,' Harry responded instantly. 'I lead my life, you lead yours. I really can't stand on the doorstep arguing with you. Go back in, Melanie. I want to close the door.'

Melanie cast Tom a pitying look. 'Why can't he come in? Or you could let him into your flat so that he could wait there.'

'I don't want him waiting for me at all! Please,' she

turned to Tom, 'if there's a shred of decency in you, just go.'

'But he's come to see you.' Melanie tugged at her elbow. 'It's all right, Harry. I'm fine here on my own.'

'Go in. *Please*.' The panic rose unmistakably in her voice. Melanie grudgingly backed the chair up, allowing Harry room to shut the door. As she closed it she stole another look at Tom's face, expecting it to be thunderous. Instead he just looked utterly weary.

'I'll wait.' His words reached her as she shut the door firmly. She leaned, weak-kneed, against the door, her heart pounding and tears pricking the backs of her eyelids. Damn him! Why couldn't he leave her alone? Why did he have to keep poking and prying? Well, now he knew it all. And what would he make of it? Let him think what he liked, she didn't care.

Melanie wheeled herself into the kitchen. 'Is he your boyfriend?' she asked. 'Have you had a row?'

'No, it's nothing like that. He's just a doctor at the hospital. We don't get on well.' Harry went over to the kitchen counter and fetched the biscuit tin, though her hunger seemed to have melted away in a storm of conflicting emotions. 'Do you want one of these? I'm starving.'

'Why don't you like him?' persisted Melanie. 'He seemed nice, except for the way he kept looking at me in this chair. You would have thought a doctor would know better than that.'

Harry finished a mouthful of digestive biscuit and sat down on the table. 'I don't think he meant to stare, he's not like that. I think he was just surprised, that's all.' She skirted round it carefully. After all, she didn't want to go raking up the past and upsetting everyone by revealing that Tom was the brother of the man whose stupidity had put Melanie in her wheelchair. 'Come on,' she said gently, 'let's finish this game before your mum and dad get back.'

They were still at it by the time Anthea and Terry returned. Harry went out to help them carry in the suitcases and camera equipment. True to his word, Tom's BMW was parked outside and she felt his eyes raking her as she greeted her friends on the doorstep. He got out of the car as she emerged from the house and stood waiting for her—like her doom, she thought dramatically when she saw him. 'Stay to supper,' suggested Anthea, oblivious to the dark figure waiting just yards away. 'We can break into the duty-free.'

Harry paused. It was tempting, but she knew Tom Buchanan well enough by now to feel certain that whatever time she finally left the sanctuary of the house, he'd still be there implacably waiting for explanations. And now he knew everything; there were no secrets left for him to discover, so she might as well get the worst over and done with. 'Thanks, Anthea, but I've got to have a talk with somebody. See you soon.' She kissed them all goodbye.

Out in the street, he was watching her like a dark shadow. She cast him a quick glance, then ran down the basement steps, aware that he was following her silently, lithe and ready to spring on her, like some jungle cat. Strangely, though, instead of being threatened, she felt a kind of calm resolve wash over her. He followed her into the flat, saying nothing.

'Before you start all over again, I need a cup of coffee,' she told him curtly, surprised at the firmness of her voice. Here in the low-ceilinged basement he seemed bigger and more powerful than ever, and that nagging, wanting feeling he aroused in her bit harder than before.

'Go ahead, I'll have coffee too.' He followed her into the kitchen, and as she filled the kettle and took the ground beans from the fridge, where she kept them, she could feel his eyes intent on her, following her every move. Awareness of him made her clumsy and she dropped the spoon as she measured the coffee into the cafetière.

'Why didn't you tell me about this?' he asked softly, breaking the charged silence. 'I'm right, aren't I? Melanie is the girl who was injured in Alex's crash?'

'Yes, you're right. I didn't tell you because there was no reason for you to know. I really don't have to explain everything in my life to you.'

'I'm quite aware of that.' He looked speculatively out into the hallway, where the toilet rolls were still stacked untidily. 'There are some things I'm not even going to ask about. But there are other questions I have to have an answer to. When did you meet Melanie?' The kettle began to boil and before she could turn it off he'd crossed the room in a single stride and lifted it from the hob. 'Why?' he persisted as he poured the water over the ground coffee. Harry felt a stab of annoyance that she couldn't even make a cup of coffee in her own home without him taking over.

Keeping her distance from him, she reached up and took two mugs from their shelf. 'Because of you,' she said, with an unexpected thrill of pleasure at the vehemence of her words, and his reaction to them. 'When you came to see me that night and told me about the accident, you blamed me for it all. You told me that if I hadn't behaved so badly towards Alex, he wouldn't have got drunk and caused the pile-up. Don't tell me you've forgotten?'

'No, I hadn't forgotten. I've often wished——' He checked himself suddenly, leaving her wondering what he had intended to say. 'That doesn't explain Melanie.' He pushed the filter into the cafetière with a force that sent the coffee spilling over the sides of the jug.

Now she'd started, Harry couldn't stop the momentum. The words came flooding out, racing over the dam that she'd so carefully constructed to hold them back. It was as much as she could do to structure them and make sense of her feelings. 'Six years ago I was a naïve little idiot, and you obviously realised how gullible I was. You took one look and then palmed off all your precious brother's guilt on me.' She slammed the coffee-mugs down on to the table. 'How could his accident possibly have been my fault? And yet you shook your finger and lectured and told me how worthless I was——'

'I was furious with you,' he admitted tersely, facing her across the narrow kitchen. 'Alex had told me——'

'Alex! That's what's so difficult for me to understand! Didn't you know your brother at *all*?' Harry could hear her own voice, scathing with pent-up fury. 'Alex would have said *anything*, anything in the world to get himself out of trouble—and you chose to believe him and blame me for it all. You came bursting in, reducing me to a pulp, and then off you went again. You ruined everything for me, but I bet it made you feel better.'

'No, it didn't,' he inserted quietly, reaching for the cafetière and placing it on the table. He sat down with slow deliberation, drawing the mugs over and filling them with coffee. Harry stared at him. He finished what he was doing, holding her in limbo until he was ready to continue. Then he looked up, and his eyes scorched her with their intensity. 'I regretted it for a very long time. I still do.'

Harry gulped, momentarily nonplussed. 'But it didn't stop you laying into me.'

'Because I was furious—more furious than I've ever been before or since.'

'I suppose that makes it all right, then.' Harry rubbed her hands in an eloquently dismissive gesture.

'Of course it doesn't. Why otherwise would I be here trying to make peace with you?' He kicked a chair out from under the table for her, plainly irritated. Harry stubbornly kept to her feet, willing him to go on. 'For your information, I felt so bad about what had happened that I came to the medical school the next week to apologise to you. By that time your Finals had started and I couldn't track you down. I wanted to see you again and prove I wasn't as unreasonable as I must have seemed that night.' He leaned towards her. 'I still want to prove it, if only you'd let me.'

The breath caught in her throat for a second. 'That's impossible.'

'I'd still like to try.' His eyes were blue Mediterranean pools, bottomless and drawing her in.

Harry stepped back and found herself up against one of the kitchen units. What did he mean? Unknowingly she ran her tongue over her dry lips. He paused, watching her, then turning to look out at the basement area through the window, wrestling with his thoughts. When he turned back to her his face was once more under control, a mask, enigmatic, unreadable.

'You still haven't told me how you come to be living in the same house as Melanie. What happened?'

'I was stupid and naïve enough to think there might have been some truth in what you said about the accident being my fault.' She measured out her words carefully; they were her only weapon in the fight against him. 'It seems incredible, doesn't it? I took everything to heart, even though I knew deep down that it was Alex who should be picking up the pieces, not me.' She gave a hollow sigh. 'As he was obviously trying to shake off his responsibilities, I decided I'd better do something about them. You'd told me which hospital Melanie was in—you made a great point of that, remember, and describing just how badly she'd been hurt—so I wrote to Anthea and Terry and asked if I could visit her. I told them who I was, how I felt that the accident had been partly my fault, and they were very nice about it.' She reached for the cup of coffee, clutching the mug for reassuring warmth.

'So that's how you got to know them. But why . . .?' Tom gestured to the flat.

'It was pure chance. I used to go and see Melanie when I could, and I visited her in Stoke Mandeville when she was transferred. We got to know each other really well and I suppose I became a friend of the family.' Harry took a sip from her mug. Her anger seemed to have seeped away, leaving her feeling chilled and empty.

'So when did you move in?'

'A couple of years ago. I really don't know why I'm telling you this,' she protested. 'It's nothing to do with you.'

'I don't agree. If it weren't for me, you wouldn't be

living here,' he said simply, his voice as smooth as dark chocolate.

'No, I wouldn't.' Harry kept the remark cold and non-committal. It wasn't that she minded being here, but it was a constant link with the past, with Alex, the accident—and the man sitting opposite her. By getting involved with Melanie, Terry and Anthea she was aware that she had merely tangled herself even more tightly in the mesh of guilt and responsibility. Sometimes she felt the urge to shake it all off, to walk away without a backward look—but that was out of the question. She'd made a commitment and she didn't intend to break it.

'You asked why I moved in. I was having trouble with the flat I was living in and around the same time Terry and Anthea were burgled. They're away a lot,' she explained matter-of-factly, 'they've got a house in the Cotswolds and another in Italy. Terry is Terry Robson—he does all those books of beautiful travel photos. After the robbery, they asked me if I'd come and live here. It seemed a good idea. I deter the burglars, lend a hand with Melanie when it's required . . .'

'And at least you can enjoy your martyrdom in comfort.' Tom slipped it in so quietly that she almost didn't hear. Harry looked at him, pale.

'That's not true. It's not like that at all.'

'No?' His voice was suddenly cynical, drawling. 'It's a very touching story, but you don't get my sympathy vote.'

'I wasn't looking for it, and I'd certainly never expect it.' Harry felt her spine turn to ice. She turned away from his penetrating eyes and put her cup down on the draining board. 'Is there anything else you'd like to know before you leave?' Her legs seemed suddenly stiff and unsteady beneath her and a vague feeling of nausea churned in stomach. There was no point in arguing with him, none at all. Whatever she said, he'd just turn her words round and use them against her.

Tom stretched, lifting his arms and extending his legs to reveal their intimidating length. 'I don't think so,' he said, studiedly casual. 'I'm beginning to understand it all. Harriet Hart—Hart by name and heart by nature. That's you, isn't it, Harry? That night I came round to tell you about Alex's accident, any normal woman would have been furious, argued her corner, insisted that it was nothing to do with her. But not you. You obviously had a guilty conscience about something, because you soaked up all the blame and then set out to turn yourself into a complete martyr.'

'Don't talk like that! You twist every word I say!' Harry whirled round on him. 'You're doing it again, just as you did that night. You're blaming me for something that I had no part in. I'm here because Anthea and Terry and Melanie are my friends . . .'

'And how many other friends do you have? What kind of life do you lead, Harry?' He leapt from the chair and stood directly in front of her, brushing her body with his own and pinning her against the unit. 'Come on, I want to hear it all. Tell me about your happy and fulfilled life, your boyfriends, your lovers——'

'No, I'm not answerable to you. You've got no right!'

'But you've just made it clear that I'm to blame for ruining your life. You've been storing up this grudge, letting it fester all these years, blaming me for your own failures. If *I* hadn't broken the news of Alex's crash like that, if *I* hadn't made you feel so guilty . . . What if,

Harry? Would things be radically different from the way they are today?' He cupped his hand under her chin and raised it.

'Don't you have any friends? No time for anyone except people you feel responsible for? Phil Beech has told me all about you—about the extra hours you put in on the ward and your willingness to come out to see the kids at any time of day or night. "I've never known such a dedicated young doctor," he told me. And he didn't know about all your good works here. He'd be doubly impressed if he did.'

She closed her eyes tight, defying him, shutting him out. 'Get out!' Her cry was anguished, breaking into a sob. The male heat of his body seemd to envelop her, surrounding, suffocating, destroying her reason. She struck out at him blindly. 'It's none of your business.'

'I think it is. No,' he said, and his voice was enough to melt her, 'I *know* it is.'

CHAPTER SIX

BEFORE she could escape, or even try to evade him, he leaned down and kissed her hard, searing her with a controlled fierceness that sent shock waves echoing through her entire body. She pushed against his chest, but it was like trying to fend off solid rock—and anyway, her spirit of resistance was juddering, trembling as badly as her hands, as she tried again to push him from her. She'd had so little experience of such things, but never had she known such overpowering male force, and from within she felt an equally strong and urgent response. It shocked her to the core to discover how hard it was to resist him. What was wrong with her that after all his insults and taunts, she couldn't muster the energy to fight back?

For a second he released her. 'Don't!' she protested, but the word came out as little more than a sigh. The pressure of his body hard against her, the musky male smell of his skin, the abrasiveness of his cheek against hers were the only things of which she was aware. Then his mouth was searching for hers again and he was gathering up her hair with one hand and caressing the nape of her neck. Harry fought her own urges, her pride and her body aching feverishly, one with desire to reject him, the other with an intense need to hold him, take from him whatever he would give her. As she summoned up the final shreds of her self-control, he lifted his head. Harry looked down at her shaking hands.

'If I didn't enjoy my work on Paddington Ward so much, you could have my notice right now.' She clenched her fists, but whom she intended to strike she didn't know. It wasn't really him she wanted to lash out at; no, there was no way in the world that she could hurt him the way he'd hurt her. The real culprit was herself and the traitorous feelings he had aroused in her.

'Right now, I wouldn't accept it.' He reached out and ran his finger slowly from her chin, along her jawline. 'Do you feel more like talking to me now, or shall I just carry on?'

Harry felt as if she'd been plunged under a cold shower. So he'd kissed her not because he'd wanted to but because he'd calculated that she would melt in his arms and become the compliant, obedient little woman he expected. 'You're a bastard,' she said icily, licking her bruised lips and finding them swollen. 'You were a bastard six years ago, and you're still one now. Nothing's changed, except that this time I'm not giving in to you.'

'So you intend to keep on fighting?' His eyes glittered dangerously.

'Yes!'

The tell-tale flush stained his cheekbones and she detected the pulse in his temple beating at speed. 'There's no way you can win,' he muttered. 'You're your own worst enemy, Harry. You make me so mad. Hell.' And this time when his lips found hers he kissed her tenderly, so softly that she was stunned. His arms enfolded her body, and this time he wasn't trapping her.

Harry fought to keep her eyes open, to remain

passive, to suppress the burning desire to respond as his lips traced a path to her earlobe. He returned to her mouth, teasing, probing, and his hands caressed her shoulders and neck, while she stood still and outwardly unresponsive, every ounce of self-possession screaming at him to stop. But he didn't stop. She could feel the heavy thud of his heart against her and hear the unevenness of his breathing. For just a second, she allowed her eyes to close, and instantly she was lost to him, her mouth opening instinctively and accepting his kisses. Her mind was numb while her body seemed to explode with unknown sensations, every nerve receptive to his touch and crying out for him.

Almost unknowingly Harry put her arms around his shoulders and clung to him as, with a sudden, shaking sob, she knew she'd clung to him in her dreams. For six years he'd tormented her, not just with his cruel words, but with the memory of his face, his body—his overpowering sexual presence. That impression of him had been just as impossible to shake off as the words he'd called her. He'd haunted her—unjust, hurtful, but capable of stirring in her feelings that no other man had ever roused. The knowledge had hurt so badly that she'd buried her feelings deep, disguising them with a thick layer of indignation and guilt, built up and nurtured every year. And now he was here again, and with unerring aim had found her Achilles heel—the only way in which she was vulnerable to him.

Almost as soon as he heard her sob, Tom pulled away. Harry's eyes were too blurred to register the shaken look on his face. 'Now we're getting somewhere,' he said, and his voice was husky. He stroked her hair back from her face as gently as he would a child's. 'Aren't you beginning to feel a little more positive about me?'

Harry came slowly to her senses, his words penetrating her fuddled brain slowly. 'No, I'm not.' She prised his hand away. 'Is this how you normally get your own way—by forcing yourself on women who don't want you?'

'Why can't you admit that you enjoyed it?' he asked brutally. 'Believe me, Harry, I know the difference between a woman who wants to be kissed and one who doesn't—and you wanted me.'

Harry tried to shape the words to deny it and found they wouldn't come. 'It was a kiss, that's all,' she said with quiet bitterness.

'Why do you keep fighting your own feelings?' he continued relentlessly. 'You can't go on denying yourself for ever.'

'Thank you, Dr Buchanan, for that patronising advice. Now you've solved all my problems, perhaps you'd like to leave. You know the way out.' Beneath the heavy layer of sarcasm, Harry felt his words burrowing like bullets straight to their target. He was right, of course; when he'd kissed her all she'd wanted to do was surrender to him, stay in his arms for ever. But what good would that have done? What would have happened if she'd given in to her desires? She shut her eyes. That way lay even more danger than she was in at the moment.

He watched her pale face fighting to conceal the pain he'd caused. Deliberately he put his hands in his pockets and stood back, reining himself in. 'Let me tell you what I see. Here you are, a caring young woman, hard-working, bright, successful——' he paused, observing her reaction, 'and seething with rage because of something that happened to you in the past. Something which you couldn't control, and for which you had no responsibility—but despite all that you stepped in and got involved. At the time Melanie and her family gave you a shield to hide behind, didn't they? No one could point the finger of blame at you, because there you were, helping out, being wonderful. The problem is, it's become a way of life for you. Melanie and her family are a nice, safe commitment—quite unlike the dangers of more intimate relationships.'

'Thanks for the psychoanalysis.' Her voice was toneless, barely concealing the fact that he'd cut her to the quick. 'Now, perhaps you'd leave.'

'I haven't finished yet.' He moved another step closer and all she could see were his eyes glowing coldly blue in the dim light. 'Outwardly everything looks fine. Good old Harry, always there in a crisis. But inwardly . . . I don't think you know how to be happy. It's safer if you don't take any risks, isn't it?'

Harry shook her head defiantly, even as her heart registered the full truth of what he was saying. 'I've never heard such rubbish.'

He seemed to ignore her. 'And I suppose you'll say that it's all my fault.'

Anger flared to life again. 'Yes, your fault, and Alex's. For once in my life I threw my cares to the wind and had a fling with your brother.' She pointed to the ceiling above their heads. 'And look what happened! You and Alex both wiped your consciences clean, but I'm different, I can't do that.'

'Maybe,' he said, his voice low and velvet smooth, 'it's time for you to accept that you've paid your debt and start again. If you'd driven the car that injured Melanie yourself and they'd gaoled you for it, you'd have been out by now. You can't allow this one sad incident to dominate the rest of your life.'

'And presumably,' she observed acidly, 'I should start this new life by kow-towing to you? Waving the white flag and pretending that we're the best of friends?'

'No!' he fired back. 'I'm not asking for your surrender or your friendship; I just want a truce.'

'So these are peace talks tonight, are they?' she laughed. 'Forgive me, but now that you've forced yourself on me, sliced my character to bits and accused me of making myself a martyr, I'm really not in the mood for negotiating a treaty. Thank goodness you didn't make your career in the Diplomatic Corps, or we would have been at war with half the world.'

He shook his head wearily. 'I'm not going to continue arguing, I've had enough for tonight. Just bear in mind that by keeping the barriers up you're straying into even greater danger. If we really can't work together, you're going to have to look for another job.' He began to walk slowly to the door, Harry sidling out of the way.

'That's blackmail,' she accused, standing well back in the dark hall as he let himself out.

He shrugged. 'What other choices do you leave me? Think about it.'

Think about it she did, incessantly, for the rest of the evening. How could he have been so cruel and destructive about her life? And how could he possibly imagine that they could work as colleagues after this? she protested to the thin air. Did he imagine that she had no pride? The memory of his kisses still burned her like a flame; she could still feel the impression of his fingers on her skin. She shuddered. Where had her pride fled to then, just when she needed it most?

Automatically, just for something to do, Harry made herself some supper but it was impossible to eat, not with her stomach heaving with a chaotic mixture of emotions. She pushed the plate away. Certain things he'd said kept floating into her mind, and one in particular stabbed her each time she replayed it. 'I don't want your friendship', those were the words he'd used. Harry buried her head in her hands, hearing it over and over again. What he wanted was something neutral. And that, she knew with a blinding ache of misery, was quite out of the question. She could hate him or . . . The tears and the realisation came together—despite everything he'd said and done, she could love him. But there was no neutral territory on which they could meet—and there was no future for her on Paddington Ward.

The next day passed in a dream. Harry felt as though she had been split into two. There was the usual Dr Hart, smiling, going through the daily routine, playing with the kids, chatting to Pat O'Brien, just as she would normally. And there was the other part of her that no one seemed to notice; the dark confusion, the whirling miasma of thoughts and emotions, racing constantly through her head, even as she stood talking to Steve Paige or a parent. She couldn't eat, and her hand trembled inexplicably when she gave Damian Potter his injection.

Worst of all was the way that every nerve in her body strained like some radar system, ready to alert her the moment Tom Buchanan came within range. It

happened just the once. She was making arrangements
with Pat for one of the children to go home for the day
for a special family celebration when her ears, as keen as
a bat's, picked up his voice approaching. He was talking
to one of the registrars and he was coming her way.
Harry thrust the form she'd just signed to Pat. 'There,
that's it. He can go home tomorrow after breakfast and
they can bring him back any time they like before eight.
Make sure the night staff know he's due back.' Before
Pat could utter a word Harry was fleeing towards
Rupert Ward. She paused as she rounded the corner,
where she couldn't be seen, and listened. He was coming
in her direction, and she heard the registrar mention the
name Patsy Cox. With a sinking heart,
Harry realised that Patsy was on this ward. She'd have
to find somewhere better to hide.

The main area of Rupert was divided into quiet glass-
partitioned sections of four beds, but off to the side
were three individual rooms where children with
infectious diseases were nursed in isolation. Harry
walked past, looking in the little windows set into the
doors. In two of them, mothers dressed in white gowns
and caps were sitting with their sick children. The third
was a twelve-year-old with meningitis. She peered in. He
was lying quietly and watching something on the far side
of the room. Harry grabbed one of the disposable paper
gowns from the cupboard outside and pulled it on,
hastily tying the tapes at the neck and waist. Then she
opened the door and slipped inside.

A nurse, attired in gown and plastic apron, looked up
from where she'd been plugging in the portable
telephone—presumably so that the patient could make a
call home. She looked surprised, but not as surprised as

Take 4 Medical Romances

Mills & Boon Medical Romances capture the excitement, intrigue and emotion of the busy medical world. A world often interrupted by love and romance...

We will send you 4 BRAND NEW MEDICAL ROMANCES absolutely **FREE** plus a cuddly teddy bear **and** a surprise mystery gift, as your introduction to this superb series.

At the same time we'll reserve a subscription for you to our Reader Service. Every two months you could receive the 6 latest Medical Romances delivered direct to your door **POST AND PACKING FREE**, plus a **free** Newsletter packed with competitions, plus author news and much, much more.

What's more there's no obligation, you can cancel or suspend your subscription at any time. So you've nothing to lose and a whole world of romance to gain!

Doctor from the Past

Your Free Gifts!

We'll send you this cute little tan and white teddy bear plus a surprise mystery gift when you return this card. So don't delay.

Fill in the Free books coupon overleaf

Reader Service
FREEPOST
PO Box 236
Croydon
Surrey
CR9 9EL

SEND NO MONEY NOW

FREE BOOKS CERTIFICATE | EXTRA BONUS

YES please send me my **4 FREE Medical Romances** together with my Teddy and mystery gift. Please also reserve a special Reader Service subscription for me. If I decide to subscribe, I shall receive 6 new books every two months for just £7.50, post and packing free. If I decide not to subscribe, I shall write to you within 10 days. The free books and gifts will be mine to keep in any case.

I understand that I am under no obligation whatsoever – I can cancel or suspend my subscription at any time simply by writing to you. I am over 18 years of age.

We all love surprises, so as well as the FREE books and Teddy, here's an intriguing mystery gift especially for you. No clues send off today!

7A9D

Name: _____
(BLOCK CAPITALS PLEASE)

Address: _____

_____ Postcode _____

Signature _____

Harry, who hadn't spotted her crouching on the floor. 'Er,' flustered Harry, 'I just thought I'd do a routine visit.'

The nurse looked at her curiously. 'Sure,' she said, 'but Steve came round about half an hour ago. There's no problem—in fact Richard's going to be transferred to Paddington this afternoon, aren't you, my love?'

The boy nodded. I was just going to ring my Dad and tell him.' Harry put her hand to her head in a theatrical gesture which she felt sure, the moment she did it, was less than convincing.

'I'm afraid Steve and I must have got our wires crossed. I thought . . . well, never mind what I thought!' She gave a dismissive laugh, aware all the while that if she walked out of the room now she'd probably find Tom Buchanan outside. 'While I'm here I might as well take a look at you,' she insisted. And despite the obvious conviction of the nurse that she'd gone quite mad, Harry spent five minutes examining the boy's chest and testing for any remaining stiffness in his neck. When she'd run through everything she could plausibly do, she took off the gown, placed it in the bin and then washed her hands with extreme thoroughness, taking as long as she could to soap herself up to the elbows. Then, fingers crossed, she left the room.

He hadn't gone, she saw immediately. He was sitting across the ward on Patsy's bed and talking to her parents. Charlie Burgess, the registrar, was standing nearby. Harry stood fixed for a second, aware that she was intended to be the third part of this team and realising just what she was in danger of losing. Working in a tight, co-operative little unit; it was the best way, she knew.

With the merest sideways look at them she hurried past. Tom saw her and for a brief moment she felt his eyes scorch her back. Then she was past them, through the doors and out into the reassuring bustle of Paddington. But the thought was less easy to flee from. It kept appearing to her like a spectre. The reality of being part of the Buchanan firm had come home to her in that split second. It was what she wanted to do. She knew now, if she hadn't before, that she didn't want to specialise in the tiny babies and endocrinology, which was what Phil Beech and Steve enjoyed so much. The alternative offer was there; everything could be perfect. All she had to do was take the risk, drop her defences, try to treat Tom Buchanan as if he wasn't a threat. And that, her sinking heart told her, was quite out of the question.

The dilemma was still preying on her mind the next day. It was her day off and as she'd been awake worrying into the small hours she allowed herself the luxury of a long lie-in. By the time she went to the kitchen to make herself coffee, Gina was already sitting there in her dressing-gown, staring despondently out of the window and stirring her bowl of cornflakes. 'Morning. I'd forgotten you were off today,' she said disconsolately, lowering her head but not before Harry noticed that her eyes were red and her cheeks blotchy. She sniffed loudly.

Weighed down with her own problems, Harry hadn't had the energy to tackle Gina's. Anyway, the girl was never here. She was still in bed when Harry set off for St Hugh's each morning, and by the time she got back Gina was gone. Harry reached for one of the toilet rolls that had been stacked precariously on top of the kitchen cupboards and tore off a long strip which she handed to her sister.

'You can start using some of this up.' Gina took it wordlessly. 'You came home early last night. It was only eleven.'

'Spying on me again?'

'No,' Harry replied tartly. 'I was in bed and I heard you running a bath, that's all. Did you have a good evening?'

'None of your business.' Gina blew her nose noisily.

'Believe me, I wish it weren't.' Harry sat down beside her and began to toy with her own bowl of muesli. She had to eat something or her body would become as weak as her mind, but every time she tried to force something down it got stuck on the lump that had developed in her throat. 'Look, Gina, I want you to phone home and tell Mum and Dad that you've given up college.'

'You're joking! They'll go mad and insist I go back home—and I'm not going.'

'You'd have a better life in Bristol than you do here,' Harry argued, aware of how useless it was going to be. 'Mum does all your cooking and washing and Dad lets you borrow the car. It's far better than being cooped up here with me, sleeping in the boxroom and lounging about all day.'

'At least you're not here to nag me all the time. That's all that happens at home—"Gina, why don't you go and do this?" "Look, my girl, you've got to do something with yourself, like Harry".' She looked mutinously at her big sister. 'Well, that's all behind me. I've left home for good. They probably wouldn't want me back, anyway.'

'Don't be stupid, of course they would.'

Gina opened her mouth as if she was going to say something, then thought better of it. Finally she muttered, 'If you're not prepared to have me here, I'll just find somewhere else.'

'Where? And how are you going to pay for it? Perhaps Paul will help out. He seems to be rolling in money, judging from the amount he can afford to waste on loo paper . . .' she stopped. The moment she'd mentioned Paul's name, Gina's face had crumpled. She mopped her tears and Harry reached for the rest of the roll. 'What's happened?' she asked gently. 'Did you have a row last night?'

'Of course we did! I don't make a habit of sitting here snivelling all morning.' Gina burst into more tears.

'What's it all about?'

There was another long pause. Twice Gina seemed about to say something but bit back the words at the last minute. She began to weep again, hiding her face in the sleeve of her dressing-gown. 'Come on,' Harry urged, 'it can't be so bad.'

'Oh yes, it *is*. For one thing, I'm never going to see Paul again.'

'Is that all it is?' Harry had said it before she'd had time to think. Compared to her own problems, Gina's seemed trivial. After all, she'd only been seeing Paul for a few weeks, and even then it hadn't seemed serious. Gina turned incredulously back to her.

'*All* it is?' She jumped to her feet. 'Is that all you can say? It's a disaster, the worst thing that could possibly happen. If only you knew!' She picked up her breakfast bowl and threw it to the floor where it landed with a shower of milk and bits of broken china dancing across the floor. Gina crunched through the remains, regardless of the mess. 'Paul doesn't want me and you obviously don't want me . . .'

'That's not true,' Harry shouted after her. 'I'm sorry you're so unhappy about Paul and I don't mind you being here, but not under false pretences, which is why I want you to phone Mum and Dad and come clean about the typing course.'

'I won't do it. You can call them and sneak on me if you want, but I'm not going to tell them.' Gina slammed out and Harry heard her retreating to the boxroom. She looked at the mess all over the floor and remembered how only a couple of days ago Tom Buchanan had stalked around in here, putting her life to rights.. Perhaps he could sort Gina's out too, she thought flippantly, and found herself almost smiling.

Outside the sun was beginning to break through the clouds for a bright and breezy day. Harry cleared up the floor and had a quick bath, ignoring the sound of the radio blaring from Gina's room. She wasn't going to hang around and let her sister exasperate her. She'd go out and give the fresh air a chance to blow her troubles away. She left a note on the kitchen table explaining to Gina where she was going and then, dressed simply in jeans, a slim-fitting black polo-necked sweater and her most expensive impulse buy, a tan sheepskin flying-jacket, she set off for Kensington Gardens.

The roses were coming into their first flowering, the buds nodding as they were buffeted by the wind, and up by the pond children were flying kites and dogs chasing balls. Harry walked briskly, feeling her blood beginning to circulate and the early summer sun on her face. It didn't stop her thinking about Tom Buchanan or mulling over his words for the millionth time, but out here in the open she felt less trapped. In the close confines of his office or the flat, even on Paddington Ward, his effect was overpowering. Coming out here into the real world reminded her that there were some things even he couldn't control, and maybe they were the best things—sunshine and wind, the happy faces of other people . . .

She sat down on a bench for a while to enjoy it all. Before long a young couple came and sat on the seat at the other side of the path. Harry watched surreptitiously as the man removed his sweater and put it around the girl's shoulders. They kissed briefly, then sat watching the world go by, holding hands and exchanging a few fleeting words, content just to be with each other. Harry got up to go and as she did so the girl looked over and caught her eye. She smiled, and her happiness was so serene and confident and obvious that Harry felt quite shaken.

What must it be like to feel so completely happy? she wondered as she walked down by Kensington Palace. And how on earth did you know when you could put your trust entirely in someone else and not be betrayed? Even Gina had more experience of such things than she did, and Gina was only eighteen! Harry kicked the gravel in self-disgust. For God's sake, she didn't want to be like Gina or some lovey-dovey girl on a park bench, she scolded herself. The minute you let yourself go and put yourself in another's hands, you risked everything. Look at Gina, crying in her room over some silly young man with more money than sense. And that girl on the seat, the chances were that her boyfriend would turn out to be an irresponsible liar or an overbearing bully. How long was her serene smile going to last?

Still smarting, Harry turned into Kensington High Street and the shops. She wasted an hour in the Next department store buying perfume she didn't need and, on impulse, a little black dress, demure but figure-hugging, with a long row of tiny mother-of-pearl buttons down the back. It was a waste of money, of course, because she'd never have an opportunity to wear it. Even so, the moment she saw it on the hanger she knew that it was right for her. As the assistant packed the dress she said laughingly, 'I hope you've got someone at home who can help you get into this—and out of it, of course. If you try to do up those buttons on your own you'll twist your back.' Her meaning was quite unmistakable. Harry smiled grimly. If she ever got the chance to wear it Gina or Melanie or Anthea could always do her up; as for undoing it, she could manage that on her own.

Emerging from the shop, Harry looked at her watch. The afternoon lay ahead of her and nothing to fill it. She could go back to the flat but she didn't want to see Gina. She could do some more window-shopping and end up with a large collection of unplanned purchases. Or she could always go and see a film, though not for an hour or two. A bus drew up at the stop and Harry recognised it as one which passed St Hugh's. Before she'd had time to think what she was doing, she was on board it and searching for her purse. Well, she rationalised, as it pulled away, she'd just go into the office and check that nothing urgent had cropped up. Tom Buchanan wasn't going to be lurking around there.

Sure enough, the office was empty when she arrived. Steve's sports gear, cricket pads and bat this time, was stuffed behind the door so that she could barely inch through. She sorted the test results on her desk. None of them was urgent—but then if they were, Steve would have seen to them. As she was finishing, he squeezed his way in.

'Harry!' He did a double-take. 'You got the message then?'

'What message?' She looked up, puzzled.

'From your neighbours, the Robinsons.'

'The Robsons,' she corrected. 'What's going on? I didn't get any message. Has something happened? Gina hasn't done anything stupid, has she?'

It was Steve's turn to look confused. 'She's the kid in the wheelchair, is she?'

'No, Gina's my sister. Do you mean Melanie? She's in a wheelchair——'

'Look, I'm not sure of the names. It's nothing to panic about. All that happened was that a couple of hours ago Mrs Robson, and her daughter in the wheelchair, came into A & E. The kid had had a fall from the chair and broken her arm or something. When they mentioned that they knew you, A & E called through to Paddington and asked if you were around—just a courtesy call. Pat said you weren't but she phoned your home and left a message there. She figured that even if you didn't catch them here, you might want to drop in once they're home and see that everything's all right.' He shrugged. 'It's something like that, anyway.'

There was a sound of scrunching paper as he trod firmly on the carrier bag Harry had left on the floor. 'What's this 'ere then?' he said in a silly accent, picking up the bag and examining it. 'Naughty undies?'

'I thought you knew me better than that,' said Harry, reaching for her handbag. 'Have the Robsons gone home yet?'

'Oh, yes, and therein lies the strangest tale of all.' He took the black dress from the bag and held it out in front of him. 'Very nice. Are the buttons at the front or the back?'

'At the back, and put it back in the bag.'

'Pity, they would have been far more exciting at the front. Are you going to wear it tomorrow?'

'Why should I wear it tomorrow?' Harry asked, annoyed. 'Look, forget that for a minute; what was so strange about the Robsons?'

Steve eyed her balefully. 'You're coming to the party, remember. The party at my house?'

'Yes, yes, I forgot,' Harry blustered. There was absolutely no point in telling him that she wasn't going. 'That's all under control, but what's this about the Robsons?'

'We-ell, who should be on Paddington Ward when this message comes through for you but ole Blue-Eyes Buchanan himself? The minute he heard your name mentioned he went haring off to A & E. Now this caused some comment, as you might imagine. After all, it's not every day a consultant volunteers to go and fix a simple fracture, is it?'

'It certainly isn't,' Harry agreed. 'Be more specific about the comment.'

'Well, there are currently two theories. The first is that Mrs and Miss Robson were his long-lost ex-wife and daughter. A little too much romantic fiction there, I reckon. The second explanation is no less gooey. Everyone's saying that the mere mention of your name drives him crazy. And I must say that gained a lot of credence when he offered to drive the pair of them home.'

'I don't believe it,' Harry muttered.

'It's true, I promise. The fact that you and the Robsons are neighbours and that it was your day off and you might be at home was not lost on the rumour-mongers in A & E. According to them, he was so desperate for a chance encounter with you that he volunteered himself as a taxi driver. Greater love hath no consultant, you have to agree.'

Harry threw her hands in the air. 'This is a nightmare! I can't believe it's actually happening.'

Steve pulled a disappointed face. 'You mean it's not true? You should try telling that to the nurse who found you trying to hide from him in one of the isolation rooms yesterday. And our teenage chess-fiend Antony told a registrar that Blue-Eyes thinks you've got great legs. Now, of course, the whole hospital knows about it. To be perfectly frank, Harry, the odds are stacking up against you.'

He leaned back in his chair, grinning at her. 'Come on, tell Uncle Steve the truth. I know you're going to be on his firm. Phil Beech took me aside and explained how the unit's going to be divided up. I hope you haven't used your feminine charms to influence the direction of your career?'

'No, I haven't—and whenever anyone so much as mentions these ridiculous lies to you, I'd be obliged if you'd squash them flat.' There was no doubting how serious Harry was. She bit her lip. 'Look, it's too complicated to explain now. You'll just have to believe me when I say that Buchanan and I get on so badly that

I can't work with him. That's why I was trying to avoid him yesterday—and he said what he did about my legs just to wind me up.'

'No, he was absolutely right,' insisted Steve.

'Thank you,' Harry said laconically. 'Now please stop larking about. Things are so bad between him and me that I'm seriously considering packing in the job.' She faltered and he waited, silent now. 'You know how much I like it here, but I really don't see any way out. The animosity between us goes too deep. He's already warned that he'll get me removed if I'm not careful. That's why I've been trying to keep out of his way.'

'Phew!' Steve let out a slow whistle. 'I knew you didn't like the man but I had no idea it had gone this far.' He shook his head reassuringly. 'Don't worry, though, he hasn't a snowball's chance in hell of getting you removed from the ward. Everyone knows you're good. Phil wouldn't let you go.'

'Maybe, but if Buchanan makes my life on this ward hell, as he's threatened to do, he can virtually force me out. It's happened before. Don't tell me you've forgotten the Wendy Savage case? A clash of personalities and wham, before you know it you're gone. So please, Steve,' she begged, 'do what you can to shut these stupid stories up. If everyone thinks it's just a lovers' tiff it makes things twice as bad.'

'All right,' he said soberly. 'But what about today? Why is he so anxious to meet your neighbours?'

Harry's mind raced. The background facts about Alex and Melanie and her own feelings of guilt were too complicated to explain, but she could see why Tom had reacted that way when he'd overheard the message. He obviously wanted to infiltrate her camp and this was his chance. He'd talk to Anthea, find out all about her helpful friend downstairs and use it as evidence against Harry. He was leaving her no corner in which to hide, no place to run to. 'It's going to sound paranoid,' she told Steve, 'but he knows how close I am to the Robsons and I think he wants to muddy the waters with them, as well as here. They're the best friends I've got. By ingratiating himself with them I suppose he intends to freeze me out.'

'Don't get me wrong, it's not that I don't believe you. You told me how you came to know him when he first arrived.' Steve had gone ominously quiet. 'But do you really think he's that calculating? If he's doing it for the reasons you think, he must be holding some immense grievance against you.'

Harry picked up the carrier bag from the desk and began the process of extricating herself from the room. 'All I've ever done to him is refuse to fall at his feet—unlike everyone else around here.' She edged round to the door. 'Look, I know to you he eems a nice guy and I realise he's making himself popular on the ward. Just don't be taken in by appearances—and warn everyone else about it too.' She left Steve sitting there, still mulling everything over.

As she'd feared, the rumours had already spread like wildfire. As she walked through the main entrance hall one of the A & E housemen stopped her. 'You must be looking for Dr Buchanan,' he announced with a sly smile.

'No, I'm not,' Harry told him curtly.

'If you change your mind he should be back any minute.' He loped off leaving Harry steaming furiously, the cynosure of a dozen pairs of knowing eyes. Her only comforting thought was the certainty that, if he knew what was being said about him around the hospital, Tom Buchanan would be even more mortified than she was. That, at least, gave her a grim satisfaction.

CHAPTER SEVEN

HARRY got out of the cab and surreptitiously checked the cars parked outside the house. There was no dark BMW—in fact no space to park so much as a bicycle. She was safe. She rang the house bell and it was opened almost immediately by Anthea, who was laughing and holding a glass of wine. 'Harry!' She kissed her warmly. 'It's all right, everyone, Harry's here!'

'Sorry I wasn't at the hospital,' Harry began, following Anthea through to the kitchen.

'No problem, we found ourselves a knight in shining armour.'

'Yes, I heard about that,' said Harry grimly. 'Just be careful not to turn your back when he's around or you'll find a lance stuck in it . . .'

Her words stuttered to a halt as she entered the sitting-room and saw the dark, long-limbed figure sitting comfortably on Anthea's Conran sofa. 'I didn't see your car,' she remarked smoothly, trying to conceal the fact that her stomach had just tied itself into a knot.

'I had to leave it round the corner,' he told her, eyeing her up and down, exploring the length of her legs, emphasised by the slim-fitting jeans. She could feel the heat of his gaze as surely as if he had touched her.

'Parking's absolutely impossible around here, except

in the evenings.' Anthea handed Harry a glass of white wine. 'Tom's been absolutely wonderful. I gather you work together?'

'Yes. Sort of. It's probably only temporary.' She shot him a split-second glance.

'That's up to you.' He raised his glass to her, taunting. 'I'd be happy to have you as a colleague.'

'Do you think you should be drinking when you're on duty?'

'*Harry*!' Anthea reproached her. 'What's got into you? I can assure you that by the time we got back we were both in desperate need of a drink.'

Tom positively exuded tolerance. 'Harry's very conscientious but she needn't worry. I'm supposed to be off-duty, but Steve called me in to look at Patsy Cox. He suspected she'd gone into renal failure.'

'Has she?' Harry asked quickly.

'It could just be retention. We'll know for certain in the next twenty-four hours.' There was a long, uncomfortable silence. Harry tried to stare at the carpet but her gaze kept straying to his legs in their casual navy chinos. Worse, her eyes kept wandering up them, noting his lean thighs and well-built torso clad in a casual, slightly crumpled fine blue and white striped shirt. It was open at the neck, and without lifting her head she could just make out the shadow of his collarbone and the strong, muscular column of his neck rising from it. She'd never paid much attention to such details except in anatomy class; never really appreciated before how deeply pleasing such conformation could be. Beautiful, even. She took a swift sip from her glass and swallowed the sudden constriction in her throat.

'Tom's been admiring your portrait.' Harry jumped,

roused from extraordinary musings.

'Oh, no, I don't think it's——' She stopped herself just in time. She'd been going to say that she didn't think it was very good; not because it wasn't an accomplished painting but because she didn't like what Anthea had seen in her. Hurriedly she changed the subject. 'Where's Melanie? Tell me what happened.'

The ploy worked. 'Melanie's having a snooze.' Anthea told the story of how Melanie had fallen from her chair as she'd been transferring from it into the car, but Harry could sense that she'd anticipated her response to the picture. Suddenly there was a kind of coolness. Anthea leaned towards Tom, smiling, utterly relaxed with him, and Harry realised with another stab of knotted anguish that they were in sympathy with each other. She was the one who was being excluded—she, to whom Anthea and Terry were like a second family, was being edged out by this newcomer.

'So Tom came to the rescue and set her arm and after all that,' Anthea finished, 'he offered to drive us home. I couldn't believe it.'

'Neither could the staff in A & E,' muttered Harry. 'They'd never seen a consultant behave so strangely before.' She glared at him. 'They suspected an ulterior motive.'

'They're right, of course.' His voice was low, faintly husky. 'As soon as I heard that Melanie and Anthea were there I had to go and see them.'

'Why?' Harry asked innocently.

Anthea let out an explosive laugh. 'Don't start pretending you didn't know, Harry! Tom's the brother of your old boyfriend—you know, Alex Buchanan, the boy who caused the car crash.' She looked at Harry in surprised amusement and tapped her sharply on the knee. 'What's got into you today? It was you who pointed out the connection to Tom in the first place.'

Harry, who'd been holding her breath for several seconds, let it out slowly. If looks could kill, Tom Buchanan would have been out cold on the sofa. 'I had no idea he'd behave so insensitively,' she apologised to Anthea. 'I thought he'd keep well away from you!' She turned accusingly to Tom. 'How could you come here, reviving old memories, stirring up things that are best left forgotten?' Her voice rose in pitch and vehemence with each word. 'Can't you understand that you can do nothing but harm here?'

Tom sprang forward, his eyes blazing blue fire and his finger pointing accusingly. 'Harry, why are you so totally determined to misinterpret everything I do?' There was an impasse. They faced each other, both bristling, like cats manoeuvring into position before a fight.

'Um—look,' said Anthea, stepping deftly into the space between them, mystified by their behaviour, 'I can understand why you should feel protective, Harry, but I really don't mind talking about the past.' She stroked Harry's hair maternally. 'I know you still feel bad about it, love, but quite frankly Terry and Melanie and I have come to terms with it. We've had to, for Melanie's sake. We had to get on with living our lives, and to do that we had to get over the bitterness. The accident was a chance in a million, but it happened to us, and we've just had to accept the fact.'

She looked thoughtfully across at Tom. 'For a time,

certainly, we thought we'd never get over it. And yes, we didn't feel like forgiving Alex. If Terry could have got his hands on him, he'd have strangled him. But time heals. We can't shoulder the grudge for ever.' She knelt by Harry's side. 'Talking to Tom this afternoon has helped fill in some of the gaps. I've always wondered what happened to Alex and now I know.'

Harry felt quite numb. How could Anthea betray her like this? After all these years when she'd stood supportively by their side, helping, protecting, never mentioning anything about the crash in case it upset them—and now Anthea was saying that none of it had been necessary. 'What did happen to Alex?' she whispered.

Tom looked at her keenly. 'I thought you were never going to ask. He bummed around for a while, then went to the States. He didn't bother sitting his medical exams. At the moment he's working in television out there. It suits him far better than medicine would ever have done.' Tom paused, trying to judge the effect it was having on her. 'He's married and they have a little girl. Unfortunately she was born with cerebral palsy—spasticity. All her limbs are affected. She's very bright, but . . .' He looked at her and she saw sadness in the depths of his eyes. 'I don't have to explain the condition to you, Harry. You know as much about it as I do.'

'So you see,' Anthea added quietly, 'Alex has as many problems as we do. More, probably. How could we possibly be angry with him, knowing how things have worked out for his own family? Tom's going to give me his address and I'll write to him . . .'

'After everything he's done to you?' Harry couldn't

hold the protest back. She felt frozen with shock.

'Perhaps you should be saying, "After everything he's done to *me*"?' It was Tom's voice, more gentle than she'd ever known it. 'It's time for you to face up to the fact that you're the only one who's keeping the anger burning. We've all found some sort of peace, all of us, except for you.'

'Only because you have no conscience,' Harry bit back.

Tom clutched his head in disbelief. 'Why on earth do you think I was so angry when I came round that night to tell you what had happened? I was furious with him and almost as furious with you. But I was mostly furious with myself for not keeping a closer eye on him.' Harry could feel something akin to panic welling inside her. He and Anthea were in league against her. He'd shoved his way in and already taken over here, manipulating Anthea, making her say these things . . .

'I knew what Alex was like,' Tom continued, and she saw the shadow of her own guilt in his face. 'I knew that if he wasn't careful he'd end up in trouble. I should have been breathing down his neck all the time, but instead I was busy with my own life.' He ran his hand roughly through his hair. 'Just like you, I blamed myself. Only it hasn't taken me six years to come to terms with the fact that nothing I could have done would have made any difference. There are so many sad and tragic things that happen in life. You really can't carry responsibility for all of them.'

Harry raised her head to glance at Anthea. 'And is that what you think I'm doing? Keeping my resentment simmering?'

Anthea put her arm round Harry's shoulder. 'Harry,

you know how very fond we are of you. You're like a daughter to us.'

Harry interrupted coldly. 'I don't want all this kindness. Please just answer my question.'

'All right.' Anthea removed her arm. 'Yes, when we first met you we realised that you felt you were in some part responsible for the crash, though we couldn't really understand why. We discussed it and decided that if it would make you feel better to get involved with Melanie for a while, there was no reason why not. And you were a great help, we couldn't have done without you. You know how much we came to rely on you.' She hesitated,

'Come on, tell me all,' Harry insisted, bright-eyed with suppressed hurt. She could feel her life beginning to crumble.

'We expected you to gradually drop out of our lives once Melanie was out of hospital and things were getting back to normal. You had your career, your friends, your life to be getting on with. But you didn't, and I suppose it was then that we realised that you hadn't got over the accident. It occurred to us that you needed us as much as we needed you. More, perhaps. Oh, Harry, I'm sorry!'

Despite her attempts to stop them, Harry couldn't prevent the tears that began to trickle down her cheek. Anthea tried to catch her in her arms, but she struggled to her feet and evaded the embrace. The tear-misted green of her eyes took Tom by surprise as she whipped round on him.

'I suppose this was what you wanted—total demolition of my life. Now you can be satisfied.'

Blinded by tears and deaf to Anthea's protests, Harry fled out of the house. She fumbled in her pocket for the keys to the flat and found instead the car keys. Yes, she thought bitterly, wiping her eyes with the back of her hand, that was better than just locking herself in the flat with Gina. She struggled to open the car door, threw her bags inside and slammed it shut after her.

Suddenly Tom was there, trying to wrench it open. Harry pushed down the lock and, ignoring him, turned on the ignition. He was shouting, and out of her rear-view mirror as she reversed, Harry could see Anthea running over.

'Don't be crazy, Harry, you're in no fit state to drive. You'll kill yourself!' His words penetrated the glass. She wound down the window a fraction and stared out into his face, his eyes almost as bright as her own. He looked genuinely alarmed. Well, good, she thought, let him worry about something for a change.

'It wouldn't matter if I did, would it?' And then she revved the engine hard and, with her tyres screeching in protest, leapt away from the kerb.

Harry sat on the end of Damian Potter's bed. It was Saturday morning and the place was pretty quiet. Those children who were well enough to go home for the weekend had left and the rest were either resting, watching the morning TV programmes or playing on the large patch of grass outside the ward windows, watched over by the playleader, parents and nurses. Damian's shoulders were hunched. He'd made another attempt to escape that morning and been brought back by the police, who had found him trying to beg money for his bus fare.

'There must be a reason why you keep trying to run away,' Harry urged. 'Don't you like it here? I thought you'd made friends—and you told me you liked the food.'

'It's all right.' He shrugged. 'I told you, I just want to be at home.'

Harry felt so tired and drained that she was quite happy to sit here patiently winkling out the problem. It seemed to her that they were both equally miserable. 'Is there something exciting going on at home? Some special event? Or maybe you want to be with your brothers and sisters?' She knew darn well he was an only child, but perhaps he'd respond to that.

'I haven't got any.'

'Are you missing your parents?' Harry checked the notes they'd made on the family and the number of times they visited. The staff of Paddington Ward kept a close eye on the number of times parents came. Mr and Mrs Potter were regular visitors. The notes also revealed that they were also married and living at the same address, important to know in these days when so many couples were divorced. It was difficult to tell what kind of pressures a separation put on a child, but sometimes it had the effect of making the kid feel unwanted. Harry had known cases before now where a child had run home because it was frightened that its parents, having split with each other, were now going to abandon it in hospital.

'No, I don't really miss Mum and Dad.' He eyed her steadily.

Harry raised her eyebrows. 'Well, I'm stumped. You like the people here, you like the food, you say that you'd prefer being here to going to school. You're not missing your mum or dad or your brothers and sisters. So there's got to be a different reason why you keep running away.' He coloured and looked down at the duvet. 'I ran away yesterday,' Harry revealed.

He was intrigued, as she'd hoped he'd be. 'Did you get far?'

'All the way to Windsor.' He was obviously impressed and asked what she'd done there. 'I walked by the river and sat and watched the ducks and the boats.' She refrained from telling him that she had sat there until it was quite dark, or that she'd contemplated chucking herself in the water.

'Why did *you* run away?' he wanted to know.

'I had a row with my friends. I wanted to go somewhere they couldn't find me. Is that why you run away?'

'No,' he said contemptuously, but there was nothing more.

'If you could get away, where would you go? Do you fancy Windsor?' He shook his head.

'I just want to get home to Hounslow. That's why I was trying to get the bus, only no one would give me any money.' They sat there silently for some time, both wrapped in their thoughts. It was eventually Mrs Potter's arrival that roused them.

Harry took her aside for a minute and explained about his latest escapade. His mum's lips pursed in exsperation. 'I really don't know why he keeps doing it,' she wailed. 'There's nothing I can think of.'

'Nothing that you or your husband have said? You haven't, for example, said that you're thinking of moving house or going away? That might make him worried that you're going to leave him here.'

'No,' insisted Mrs Potter, racking her brains, 'nothing at all. As if we'd even dream of moving or going away with him in here!'

'I've probably asked you this already, but does he have a dog or a cat? Anything that he might be missing?'

'No!' she shook her head. 'Nothing like that at all. Well,' she said after a moment's thought, 'there's his rabbit—but he doesn't normally take much notice of it. I'm the one who has to keep cleaning out the hutch.'

Harry grinned. 'You never know, it could be the clue we're looking for. It's funny the things kids miss when they're away from home. Tell you what, offer to bring him a picture of the rabbit and see if he takes any interest at all. If he does, I think we've struck gold. Let me or Sister know and we'll try and fix something.'

'Could I bring the rabbit in with me?' asked Mrs Potter.

Harry frowned. 'We've had dogs and cats come to visit before now, and frankly it hasn't gone down well. The cat ran away and couldn't be caught and one of the dogs got fed up with all the attention and snapped at someone. I'd have to get permission from my consultant.' Those last two words made her heart jump. She'd said them without thinking, but her consultant these days was Tom Buchanan, not reliable old Phil Beech. 'You find out whether the rabbit holds the key to Damian's anxieties, and if it does, I'll find some way of getting it in. OK?' Mrs Potter agreed and went striding off to do her piece of detective work.

Harry wandered aimlessly round looking for something to do and not finding it. If only she was busy she wouldn't have so much time to think. Unfortunately things were extremely quiet. Miraculously all the babies on Teddy Ward were quiet. Even Patsy Cox, whose condition had been giving cause for concern, had made a startling change for the better. Harry checked her drip for the dozenth time. Patsy's mum, who'd been sitting up with her most of the night, had gone for a nap, so Harry stayed to read a story. Normally she liked to make the tales as funny as possible, with the addition of silly voices and noises, but as her patient was already in stitches she kept it calm. Just before she got to the end Patsy, who'd been listening intently, saw someone coming past behind them. She raised her hand in a weak wave. Harry, not bothering to turn round, smiled.

'Who was that, one of your friends?'

'Yes.' Her pretty face lit up. 'Dr Tom.' Harry's own face must have betrayed something because Patsy added, 'He's nice, isn't he? The nurse was saying that he's your boyfriend. I wonder why he didn't come over?'

Harry cleared her throat. 'I expect he didn't want to disturb us.' She finished the story slowly and sat with Patsy for another ten minutes until she fell asleep. Then she slipped quickly back to Paddington Ward, told the duty sister that she was going home and, checking that she'd got her bleeper, left the hospital.

Gina was sitting on the sofa in her dressing-gown and watching the Saturday afternoon horse-racing when she got back. For once she seemed in a good mood. 'Hi! No one at death's door?' she greeted her big sister.

'You have such a charming way of putting things.'

'Sorry. Are all the little darlings tucked up tightly in their beds?'

Harry sighed. 'One day I'll take you in and you can see for yourself. In their beds? You obviously subscribe to the Victorian view of paediatrics.'

Gina suddenly sat up. 'There was a call for you. A man, I wrote it down.' She ambled off to the kitchen. Harry tried to quell the iron fist that was thrashing around inside. Only one man sprang into her thoughts, and why would he call her? What was there left to say?

'It's from Steve Paige. He says if you're not there tonight by nine-thirty he'll come and drag you there himself. He left his address, too. He's in Notting Hill.' Gina handed her a slip of paper. 'I hope it makes more sense to you than it does to me.'

Harry breathed a sigh of relief. 'He's having a party.'

'That'll be nice for you. Are you going to wear that new dress you bought yesterday? I'm sorry!' she said when Harry looked threateningly at her. 'You left the bag in the hall when you came in last night and I couldn't resist taking a look.'

'No, I'm not wearing it—because I'm not going.' Harry changed TV channels. As usual on a Saturday afternoon there was nothing but sport and black and white cowboy movies. She turned it off.

'You got the message. If you're not there by nine-thirty he's going to come round and be masterful,' Gina warned.

'Steve! He's not the masterful type,' laughed Harry at the very thought.

'You're joking! He's gorgeous—at least, he seemed pretty impressive yesterday afternoon.' Gina was looking at her with new respect. 'I heard you yelling at him and then doing your impression of Nelson Piquet, roaring off down the road. He hung around for hours afterwards, talking to Anthea and waiting for you to come back. It was dark by the time he left. He was here again this morning, too.'

'That's not Steve,' corrected Harry, the hair on the back of her neck standing on end. 'This man, the man outside yesterday—you didn't talk to him?'

'No, he didn't knock. This morning he drove up looking for your car and when he didn't see it he went to see Anthea again. I heard him asking whether you'd come back last night and when she said you had, he went off again.' She winked. 'He's obviously after you.'

'God, yes, he's after me all right. But not for what you think. He's after my blood.' She drummed her fingers on the coffee-table. 'If he ever comes here, Gina, I'm out. Just shut the door on him, understand? Even if I'm hiding behind you, I'm out to him.' He could come at any time, Harry realised, and she had no defence. He knew where she lived and worked. He knew almost everything about her life. He might come looking for her again tonight. Her only hope of getting away from him was to go somewhere unpredictable, somewhere he couldn't find her.

'Maybe I will go to that party,' she said aloud. 'I'm on call all weekend but if I take my bleep it should be OK. Steve's only just up the road, so it won't take more than a few minutes to get back to the hospital if I'm alerted.'

'You can wear that black dress, and I've got some nice dangly pearl earrings that'll match the buttons,' Gina offered. 'And I'll do your hair in a French plait, the way I did the other day. It looks really good like that.' She grinned. 'No one's going to believe it when they see you done up to the nines.'

'It'll certainly be a surprise,' agreed Harry. She turned to her sister. 'And it's good to hear you sounding so much better. Have you made it up with Paul?'

'No.' Gina took a deep breath and went to say something, but it still wouldn't come. 'No,' she repeated. 'I'm going to have to cope without him. I'm old enough to look after myself, anyway, no matter what happens.'

'Good, I think you're right. Men—who needs them anyway?' Harry managed a laugh, though inside she felt far from amused.

CHAPTER EIGHT

THERE was no mistaking Steve's house. The lights flooded the small front garden and music permeated the open windows. Harry paused on the path, gathering the courage to knock. Suddenly she felt uncomfortable in her black dress and flashy earrings and the make-up that Gina had applied. It looked good, that she'd had to admit. The dress was very flattering, demure but sexy, clinging to her breasts and waist and hips and skimming above her knees. Gina had used dark shadow on her lids and a russety blusher that Harry wouldn't dared have touched, and somehow they'd made her appear much more dramatic and exotic than usual. That was the problem. She wasn't dramatic and exotic by nature and she felt a fraud. She was dressed up as someone else, not herself.

As Harry stood hovering, a couple came up the path behind her and rang the bell. They smiled and said hello and before she had a chance to escape the door opened and Steve spotted her. He looked her up and down approvingly but all he said was, 'I'm glad I didn't have to force you to come. Come and meet some of my friends.'

Quaking inwardly, Harry followed him through the crowd. He introduced her to one of the people he shared the place with and a huge, blond Australian man with the tanned good looks of a surfer. Before she knew what was happening, Harry was in conversation with them. Another man, a journalist, joined the group and then Pat O'Brien came over with her companion. They circulated, talking and drinking, and Harry couldn't quite believe how easy it all was. She'd been to very few proper parties in her life. At college and later at the hospital where she'd done her two years as an intern, parties had been an excuse to escape from the hard work and long hours. The drinking had been hard, the music loud, the lights low and talking had been one of the last activities on the agenda. She'd felt threatened by the close dancing with men she hardly knew and the things they'd muttered to her in the dark. Compared to them, Alex had been relatively sophisticated. He'd made her laugh first, treated her like a real person, broken the ice with silly stories and flattery, and only then had he asked her to dance. After that . . . Harry deliberately blanked out thoughts of what her meeting with Alex had eventually led to. Not tonight, not while she was enjoying herself.

But why on earth had it taken her so long to realise that parties didn't have to be like that? she wondered as she was introduced to yet more new faces. People were beginning to go off together and dance in the other room, but when the Australian asked her to dance with him and she turned him down with a smile, he didn't seem to mind. Harry could barely believe it. This was actually fun.

She was well into an avid discussion about the ethics of using animals in medical research when she became aware of someone hovering at her elbow, looming above her. She looked up, laughing, expecting to see the Australian who seemed to have taken a fancy to her.

Instead she found Tom Buchanan's blue eyes focused directly upon her. The laughter froze on her lips. She turned swiftly back to the couple she'd been talking to, but the spell had been broken and in that instant all her self-consciousness and doubts came flooding back. She couldn't think what it was she'd been about to say to them and, anyway, her vocal cords seemed to have undergone some kind of paralysis. But that was as nothing compared to the sudden blind panic she felt overtake the rest of her. Her heart began to race uncontrollably and her stomach became an aching void once more. She stared desperately at the carpet, trying to control her body which seemed to have taken on an independent life of its own.

Tom smiled at the rest of the group, who couldn't help but notice how Harry's face had dropped. With devastating charm he introduced himself to them. 'I'm afraid I've taken Harry by surprise,' he added with laconic amusement. 'She was beginning to think she was safe here.'

He was reading her mind now! Harry ignored the provocative remark. Out of the corner of her eye she could see the blond Australian standing in the hallway. 'Excuse me,' she said quickly, 'but I have to go and speak to someone.' Without a backward glance at Tom, she eased her way through the packed bodies and out into the hall. 'If you'd like to dance now, I've changed my . . .' She faltered, suddenly realising that her Antipodean admirer had his arm round the red-headed woman at his side. Harry was flustered. 'I'm sorry, I didn't see . . .' She turned round blindly and crashed straight into a male chest. Tom Buchanan's male chest. Harry knew it without looking up. She knew the smell of him, clean, slightly tangy, and with the individual undertone of male muskiness. She knew the way their bodies fitted together, her head just level with his shoulder, her cheek pressing against the warm firmness of his pectorals.

'I'll dance with you.' His arm closed firmly about her shoulder and Harry felt she'd buckle under the weight of it, so weak was she feeling.

'No, I don't . . .' she muttered, but he silenced her with a swift, gentle kiss.

'Don't do that! Everyone will see!' she protested.

'Come and dance then.' He manoeuvred her towards the back room where one other couple were smooching to slow music, deeply preoccupied with each other. There was no time for Harry to object—and anyway, by doing so she'd just draw more attention to herself, she knew. In the dimness of the room he held her close, one arm around her waist, the other securing her shoulder. Harry leaned back, putting as much space as possible between their bodies, her head upright, her eyes challenging him. She kept her hands hanging by her sides. Nothing would made her cling to him, she resolved, the fire in her beginning to flare and consume her fear.

'Why are you doing this?' She modulated her voice so that only he could hear.

'Dancing? Because I enjoy it. It's even better if my partner enjoys it too,' he said lazily, his blue eyes on slow burn. 'Relax, Harry, and you'll understand what I mean.' He guided her backwards and for a moment the full length of his body came into contact with hers. Harry felt a shudder of reaction, a spiralling awareness of the unmistakable masculinity of him.

'I have no intention of relaxing for a moment,' she rasped. 'Why won't you leave me alone? You keep spying on me—at the hospital, at Anthea's—and now here!'

'I just wanted to make sure you were all right.' She felt his arms contract, holding her more tightly, and his blue eyes glowed like sapphires.

'Very funny,' Harry snarled, and she placed her palms hard against his chest and pushed him away, deliberately treading on his feet as she did so. 'How can you be so completely hypocritical? After all the things you said yesterday—the things you made Anthea say!' She had to stop and swallow the sob that was welling in her throat. 'And then you have the nerve to say you wanted to make sure I was all right? You don't give a damn about me!'

'If only that were true!' It was scarcely more than a sigh and Harry wasn't sure she'd heard it properly. As if he'd been just toying with her so far, allowing her to think she could keep him at arm's length, he suddenly pulled her to him and she realised, not for the first time, that she was completely powerless against his brute male strength. 'God, if only that were true,' he repeated, this time breathing the words into her ear. She could feel his fingers gently stroking the nape of her neck, his hand in the small of her back pressing her to him. 'You're making me crazy, Harry, and I don't know why. All this aggression and anger, and yet . . .' he kissed her neck, his tongue tracing a meandering line up and down, from her collarbone to her ear.

Harry felt a tremor starting at the base of her spine and working up, making all her nerves scream with aching, pulsing desire. 'I hate you.' Her voice sounded rusty and unfamiliar. 'You're just like Alex.'

He raised his head, and she saw his lips compress and his eyes assess her brilliantly through mere slits. 'You know that's not true. I'm nothing like Alex.' He ran the pad of his thumb across her top lip, seeming to absorb every detail of her face. 'Look at me and tell me you hate me.' He held her head so that she couldn't turn away. 'That's all you have to do, Harry. Look me in the eye and say it. They're your magic words for freedom. Say them and I'll just walk out of here.'

Harry licked her lips. 'I . . .' She shut her eyes, barricading herself against that all-seeing blueness. 'I hate you.'

'And now with your eyes open. It's easy.' He'd released her, she realised. He was standing still in front of her, waiting.

She tried again but the words wouldn't come. Something else kept rising up and blocking them each time she tried to utter them. 'I . . . I can't. You know I can't.'

'And neither can I. You're the most impossible woman I've ever met, you've put me through hell—and yet hate's the last thing I feel.' They stood there, two feet apart, just gazing at each other. Harry felt feverish, as if she was surviving on pure instinct. 'What are we going to do?' he asked quietly.

She shook her head. 'I don't know.' She looked round. Other people had come in but they were dancing, absorbed in each other and not paying too much attention to what was going on. 'I don't want to stay here.'

'All right.' He put his arm protectively round her waist. 'Let's go.' For once his touch did not incite or inflame her. It felt absolutely right as he guided her out of the house, past Pat and Steve, who wisely said nothing and refrained from exchanging knowing smiles until after the front door was firmly shut again.

'Your place?' Tom asked, turning the car into Notting Hill Gate.

'My sister's there.' Harry realised with a shiver that for the first time she was seeking to be alone with him. Before she had done her best to avoid such a confrontation. Without a word he drove on towards Holland Park, then turned left and finally parked in Campden Hill Square. Harry had been there before, but just as a sightseer. It was one of the more exclusive parts of west London, its elegant houses inhabited by a variety of famous names.

'Come in. The place is a tip at the moment, it's had to be rewired, replumbed, replastered—everything.' There was no carpet in the hall and the walls were bare, raw plaster. Harry absorbed it without seeing. She didn't know what was wrong but she seemed to be in a dream, gliding along almost effortlessly, not thinking, just feeling. The place echoed to their footsteps. 'This is a little more comfortable.' He led her through to a large room at the back, bare and echoing again, but in the middle of the floor was an Indian carpet and on it a huge old sofa and a low coffee-table with a lamp. It was, she guessed, the place where he lived and worked in the middle of the disorder. Scattered around this island of comfort were cardboard boxes and a stereo, its wires trailing snake-like across the floor.

Tom flicked on the lamp. It created a circle of light in the middle of the sea of floorboards, leaving the bare walls unseen. He walked over to the window to close the

wooden shutters. Harry watched him closing her in,
hiding her from the world, making them completely
private. Her thoughts began to stir and a faint alarm
bell began to ring somewhere in the back of her head.
What had she done? She'd surrendered to this man,
shown the white flag and given in, despite her vows to
fight on. He was coming back towards her now, and
there was something in his eyes that she couldn't bear to
see. She looked around for some kind of distraction.
The box near her feet seemed to contain photos. She
dropped to her knees and began to look through them.
'These look interesting.' She could hear the nervousness
in her own voice.

'They're pictures of my kids.' He moved over to the
stereo and she watched him put on a compact disc.

'You've got children?'

'No,' he shook his head, smiling slightly. The strains
of a Bach violin concerto, the one to which she did her
yoga, began to resound gently around the room. 'The
kids I've treated. Most of them there are successes.
When we've got the unit going properly and I've got a
consulting-room, I'll put them up in there. It gives hope
to parents whose own children are sick.'

Harry looked through them, dozens of pictures of
different children, some with parents and brothers and
sisters, some on their own, some with their favourite
nurses. Some looking healthy and smiling, others thin
and bald and still smiling broadly. Tom came and sat
behind her on the carpet, looking over her shoulder as
she turned over picture after picture. He named each
child and described its problem without hesitation. She
reached the end of the pile and sat holding the last
picture. He took it gently from her hand and put it back

in the box. 'And now . . .' He stood up and lifted her to her feet. They stood facing each other, touching as they had at the party.

Harry found herself unable to move, as if she was caught in a dream. All she could see were the blue flickers of desire burning in his eyes as he bent to kiss her. Any protest she had been about to make died as she felt a reciprocal tugging at her. She shut her eyes and surrendered to him, opening her mouth, tasting his tongue on her lips. It was no defeat. The world exploded into a new realm of physical sensation and she knew, instinctively, that the more she gave in to him, the more she would discover. The skin of his neck was smooth and firm and hot as she explored it with her hands and lips. The evening growth of beard on his chin rasped her as they kissed, and she could feel the tight cords and the pulse at his throat as vividly as if they were her own. Her hands explored his spine, thrilling at the sheer strength and solidity of the muscles in his shoulders.

She opened her eyes for a second and found dark, wanting passion staring back at her from his. Which of them groaned as his hands began to undo the tiny mother of pearl buttons down her back, she didn't know. This was how it had been in her dreams; this was what she had been fleeing from for so long without really understanding. That first time she'd met him, she's known that he held this power over her and that to him her surrender would have to be complete. She stood still now, her cheek pressed to him, aware of his uneven breath, wanting to feel his hands on her bare skin. He undid each button slowly, teasingly, running his fingers lightly over each newly exposed vertebra, kissing her neck and mouth, driving her wild with an aching desire she'd never known before. All caution thrown to the winds, Harry began to undo his tie and the buttons of his shirt, running her hands over the taut firmness of his chest, wantonly licking and kissing the hot velvet of his skin.

He moaned her name, taking her face softly in his hands, caressing her cheeks and kissing her again, more deeply still, so deeply that she forgot who she was and where she was and praying for the sensual darkness to overtake her. Wordlessly he led her to the sofa. He sat down and cradled her, half sitting, half lying, in his lap, kissing her, exploring her contours with his hands, running his fingertips over the delicate lines of her neck and shoulders and the pliant softness of her breasts, still covered in fabric. When she could bear it no longer Harry helped him softly tug down the top of her dress, easing her arms out of the sleeves. She wore no bra and yet she felt no shame or embarrassment about revealing her body. All that had gone, been burned up by something more consuming. She wanted him to touch her, take her, put an end to the aching and emptiness that was racking not just her body but her life.

She watched his reaction as the slim-fitting bodice fell away and revealed her softly rounded breasts, her nipples already full and hard before his lips and exploring hands found them. He murmured her name as he bent to taste her, and at his first touch she felt something snap in her, the last vestiges of self-control. She had no experience or knowledge to guide her, just pure instinct. The pulsating male scent of him aroused her to frenzy. She pulled at his shirt and for a moment he tore his attention from her body and helped her remove it. Then they were a tangle of arms and legs, mouths seeking each other, his hands touching her in places no man had touched her before, she shamelessly exploring him, discovering for the first time the delights of the male body, her nails raking him, his mouth possessing her breasts, first fiercely, then softly. She arched her back, pressing herself against him, aware of his hard arousal and wanting him with an agonising, abandoned ache.

'Not here.' His voice was thick, tortured by desire. Somehow he scooped her up and carried her across the dimly lit room, kissing her all the while, pressing her bare torso to his. Harry could feel his muscles clenching and the sweat breaking out on his skin. She leaned down and opened the door. It swung open easily and she knew as it did so that she was sealing her own fate. There was no going back now. He carried her up the stairs, pausing half-way to take her breast again and tug softly at its aching tip with his teeth.

Harry moaned and clutched him tighter, willing him to take her now, quickly, before she died of this sensual agony. The empty house echoed to her groan. The compact disc had finished. It was silent except for the uninhibited noises of their passion. She ran her fingertips round his lips, and he took her fingers in his mouth and sucked them as he had her breast. He began to climb the stairs again, his eyes fixing hers so that she was unable to look away, and despite the savage wanting in his face she saw a new and unexpected tenderness. 'You can trust me,' he said quietly as they reached the landing and stopped. 'I'm not like Alex.'

She remembered when he'd talked about his patients, the kids whose lives he'd saved and those he'd fought for and lost. Something came over him when he discussed them, something unbearably intense yet so gentle—the combination of toughness and caring that made him such a good doctor. He was prepared to hurt them, poisoning them with toxic chemicals, if it made them better in the long run. They put their trust in him. In his eyes now she saw that same look, the willingness to take responsibility and fight to make things right.

'I know I can trust you,' she said, stroking his shoulder and suddenly feeling shy. 'I didn't sleep with Alex, you know. I haven't trusted anyone enough for that.'

He smiled so softly she knew her heart would break. When it came, his kiss was so tender she felt herself weightless and dissolving in his arms. He pushed open one of the panelled doors with his foot and she could see the bed, large and covered with an antique hand-stitched white quilt, illuminated by the moonlight streaming in through the window. As he took the first step a noise broke the silence of the house, distorted and echoing among the empty rooms but its pulse and pitch quite unmistakable.

'God, no, not now!' He bent his head and she felt the coarseness of his hair tickling against her breast. Harry struggled in his arms.

'It's my bleep. I felt it in my bag on your sofa.' As if she'd suddenly woken from a dream she prised herself from him. He let her gently down to the floor, his hands running softly over her warm skin. 'Where's your phone?' She could barely speak when he touched her like that.

'Downstairs.' He walked down in front of her, switching on the lights and destroying the gloomy atmosphere with the brilliance of the hundred-watt bulbs. He led her to the room with the sofa. The phone was on the floor behind it and Harry picked it up and dialled the number. The bleep stopped as she got through and was transferred to Rupert Ward.

Suddenly, as she waited for the connection, she became aware of her nakedness. With one hand she attempted to pull on the top of her dress, noticing as she did so the pink marks gleaming across her skin, showing where he had kissed and nibbled at her flesh. As she was struggling, Tom's firm hands took over, holding out the sleeves for her to slip her arms into, and smoothing the bodice up over her breasts with a touch that still managed to inflame her. For a second she placed her free hand over his, pressing it to her for reassurance. It was he who pulled away and, after silently kissing the nape of her neck and running his tongue the length of her exposed spine, began the job of buttoning it up.

It seemed an age before Night Sister came to the phone. 'Come on!' Harry protested, praying that it was a false alarm and they'd be allowed to start again where they had left off. Across the room she watched Tom pick up his shirt and put it back on. He walked towards her, raising an eyebrow enquiringly, the light still burning in his eyes. Harry shook her head to indicate that nothing was being said and with brazen confidence inserted her hand under the shirt, feeling the silky smoothness of him and the firmness of his muscles taut beneath his golden skin. She'd never known such sensuality, such overwhelming desire. Silently she tried to indicate that he didn't need to do up his shirt—not yet, anyway. Tom smiled indulgently and kissed her ear, but started fastening the buttons nevertheless, and she had to pull her hand away.

'Hello, Sister! You bleeped me?' There was a five-minute conversation.

'OK,' Harry ended it, 'but let me know if it happens again and I'll come in and resite it.' She put the receiver down.

'No major alert?' Tom had tucked his shirt into the waistband of his chinos. Both of them stood there, neat and tidy, every button secure and nothing, except the beating of their hearts and the burning warmth of their skin, to indicate to the world what had been happening just five minutes earlier.

'Patsy Cox's drip stopped working. Sister called the duty officer some time ago but he was so busy that in the end she had to alert me. At which point,' Harry cast him a meaningful look, 'he promptly turned up and fixed it.' She looked up, her eyes glowing as she thought of what they might have been doing now if the bleep hadn't gone off, to find a new coolness in his face. There was a long silence, during which the charged atmosphere of the room seemed to evaporate. Once more it was rather cold, empty and echoing. As if a magic spell was wearing off, Harry was suddenly aware of the bare boards and the smell of paint. She felt her body, so magically alive and supple and responsive to his touch, become cool and defensive. A twinge of embarrassment replaced the uninhibited burning she'd felt only minutes before.

He picked up his jacket which had fallen to the floor and took out his car keys. 'I'll drive you home.'

Harry caught her breath. That old, familiar steel bar was back churning in her stomach, making her feel sick and heavy, smashing a great hole in her abdomen. 'I left my car at Steve's,' she managed, while her heart and

every other part of her screamed another question—
Why?

'I'll take you back to Notting Hill.' He looked away,
brushing his hand through his hair, smoothing out a
ruck in the carpet with his foot. Harry was rooted to the
spot, the pain grinding inside her.

'I thought . . .' She had to swallow. 'I thought we
were going to . . .' She couldn't say it.

He looked across at her swiftly. 'So did I, but now,
well . . . my better self has asserted itself. It would have
been a mistake. I can't exorcise my ghosts like that.'

It took Harry a few moments to appreciate what he
was saying. The truth dawned suddenly. 'So that was it?
It was just a way of getting Alex and the past behind
you. You've already taken out your anger and
frustration on me. All that was left was to lay me and
the ghost at the same time?' she added, surprised at her
own crudity.

'No, no . . .oh, I don't know, something like that,
maybe.' He hid his confusion by turning briskly
towards the door. 'And if you're honest, that probably
goes for you too. I can't explain it, Harry, except to say
that we're involved for all the wrong reasons, not the
right ones.' He shook his head hopelessly. 'If you were
experienced, if you'd had lots of lovers, maybe I'd feel
you were fair game.' Distractedly he ran his hand across
the back of the sofa, trying to control his breath. 'But
that's not the way things are. I've never thought of
myself as a romantic, but for your first time you deserve
something better.'

Harry was shaken to the marrow. She'd wanted him
more than anything in the world. She'd wanted his sex,
to feel him inside her, filling the aching loneliness of her

life. She'd been wanting him since that first night they had met. Yes, she could admit that now. The knowledge hadn't been so explicit then, her anger and her wanting were too confused, but tonight she'd been without doubts. Tonight she'd thought she understood what she felt for him. Foolishly, ridiculously—for all the wrong reasons as he'd said—she had acknowledged her love. And, with his unerring sense of what would hurt her most, he had rejected it.

'For your own good, Harry, let me take you back to your car. You've already got a dozen good reasons for disliking me. If you stay you'll end up with another.'

Harry froze. 'And if I go I'll have one too.'

He looked at her and she saw something tortured in his face. 'All right, stay if that's what you really want.' By the time he'd finished the words he was across the room, kissing her savagely, one hand behind her head while with the other he found her breast and his thumb circled her nipple hard and bruisingly. Harry tried to struggle but he pinned her hard against him so that she felt the full proof of his arousal. Finally, after what seemed an eternity, he lifted his head and let her go. They were both breathing heavily. 'There, is that what you want?' he asked, his voice almost slurred. 'Nothing better than that? I'd be only too happy to oblige, but the responsibility is yours alone. If you regret it later you can't blame me. I refuse to accept responsibility for causing you any more unhappiness.'

That wasn't what she wanted, Harry knew. She wanted his tenderness, the warmth that melted her resistance—not this overpowering display of strength. 'You told me I could trust you,' she said accusingly.

'In the heat of the moment, that was all.' His mouth

twisted in pain. 'Look, don't trust me. Never trust me. That way you'll be safe. Let's forget all this and behave towards each other as professionals. No talk of the past, or how we feel. Just paediatrics. Not a word more.'

'That's fine by me. It's what I've wanted all along,' Harry said flatly, her tone valiantly concealing what she felt. So she was to forget what he'd said about wasting her life, forget the way he'd muscled in on the Robsons, pointing out her weaknesses and dependency on them? And she was supposed to forget what had happened here between them tonight? All right then, she'd do it. She would be as tough as he was, every bit as cool and calculating and destructive.

She picked up her bag which was on the sofa. 'Perhaps you'd call me a cab, then, so that I can get back to Notting Hill.'

'I'll run you there myself.'

'Oh, no,' Harry shook her head warningly. 'This is strictly business, remember? No little favours. I don't want you to think I'm depending on you in any way.'

'If you insist.' He made the call. Harry waited by the front door until the taxi came, listening to the sound of Tom's footsteps echoing up and down as he paced the floor of the room. She opened the door the instant she heard the familiar diesel tickover of the black cab. He came out on to the pavement and held open the door as she got in. Steeling herself, Harry held out her hand. He took it and apparently without thought stroked the inside of her wrist, making shivers run all the way up her arm. Harry grabbed it back quickly.

'Well, goodbye, Dr Buchanan. I expect I'll see you at work.'

'Harry, I didn't mean it to be like this,' he started, but she slammed the door and the rest of his words went flying, unheard, into the night air.

CHAPTER NINE

IT WAS extraordinary what a difference fourteen days could make, Harry thought as she left Paddington for the walk to Outpatients, where she had a clinic starting at nine. Two weeks ago she'd been happy in her life and work, little suspecting that trouble was just round the corner. One week ago she'd been a miserable wretch, covered in shame and aching with a pain that wouldn't leave her, convinced that her life had fallen to pieces. She'd been caught crying in the loo by one nurse and Steve had tactfully taken to knocking firmly on the office door before entering in case he disturbed her. And this week? Well, she was thinner. The looseness of her skirt waistband told her that. She was pale, too, and her eyes were shadowed and dark. Half the staff of the hospital seemed to have commented on it, many of them with knowing smiles. And there was about her a new quality—a steelier look in her eye and a firm set to her mouth. She didn't smile or joke as much as she used to, and she said very little to anyone, not even to Steve or Pat O'Brien.

She'd changed officially, too. Now she was houseman on Tom Buchanan's team, working in tandem with Charlie, the registrar. Though how long that was going to last, Harry wasn't sure. To say that it was a strain to see Tom almost every day, to report to his office with notes and information, to stand with him, pretending to be smiling and relaxed as he conducted a formal ward round or spoke to parents, was a massive understatement. She coped by being supremely professional and avoiding his eye whenever possible. And never being alone with him. There was no fight or spark left in her. Her anger and frustration were turned inward on herself as she reassessed the things she'd done and said over and over, replaying them like a video and never getting much sense out of it.

He was, she sensed, as uncomfortable with her as she was with him. They communicated the bare medical facts in professional jargon, briskly, and with so much tension in the air that no one could ignore it. 'You two are frightening the parents,' Pat O'Brien complained one afternoon. 'You should have heard the Morrises after you and Tom had explained about fixing their baby's cleft palate. Mrs Morris was convinced something was terribly wrong, and when I asked how she knew she said it was because you two were obviously trying to hide something.'

Harry's response had been brief and unfriendly. 'If it happens again,' she'd snapped, 'you can always tell the parents that we don't get on. In fact I dare say you can supply them with graphic details of the whole sordid business.' She'd walked away, leaving Pat open-mouthed and rightly angry. They hadn't made it up with each other yet.

As if all that wasn't enough, she was worried about Gina. When she'd got home yesterday evening there had been no sign of her and she hadn't come back last night. Harry had checked her room only quickly, but she felt pretty sure that Gina's red overnight bag had gone. She'd left no note, not a word of explanation—but then, Harry thought, kicking herself, she'd hardly been in the mood to listen. Maybe she could go home early this afternoon after the morning's Outpatients clinic and see if Gina was back.

Normally she didn't do much Outpatients work, but Charlie, the registrar, was off on a day's course and Harry was handling his clinic. Most of the cases were follow-up checks on children who had already been seen, and the majority of new referrals would go to Tom Buchanan. This morning they'd be working in tandem, she dealing with the strictly routine patients while he saw those with complications. If she encountered any difficult cases she'd have to inform him. Harry crossed her fingers that it would be a dull and boring morning.

And so it was. The first sixteen cases were all straightforward, including a check-up on a child who had had acute renal failure and a girl with a slight heart murmur who came in every few weeks to have it monitored in case it worsened. At lunchtime the final patient was a three-year-old boy referred by his GP because of weakness in his legs.

The mother brought him in and he sat quietly on her lap as she explained the problem. 'He started walking at around the right age, but recently for some reason he's been getting very clumsy. He keeps falling over and hurting himself, as if he's getting weak,' she said. 'We had his eyes tested because we thought it might be that, but they said he was all right.'

Harry smiled reassuringly. 'Well, in that case we need to start looking for some other cause.' She ran through her list of routine questions about the child's development and habits and the rest of the family, just to get a good background knowledge of the situation. It all seemed normal and her quick examination of him showed no obvious signs of trouble. 'Come and sit down on the floor, Matthew,' she suggested, sliding off her own chair and kneeling on the ground. She clinked some yellow plastic bricks together and, forgetting his shyness, he came over to play with her.

Harry watched, talking in relaxed tones to both mother and son. His co-ordination was good and his speech quite advanced. Already a diagnosis was beginning to shape itself in her mind. All she needed was a final test. 'Matthew,' she called, holding a fluffy teddy bear above his head. He looked up and tried to grab it but she raised it higher, making him get to his feet. He struggled to do so, placing his hands on his knees and gradually moving up to his thighs, forcing his body slowly upright. It was a difficult manoeuvre.

'You see?' said his mother.

'Yes, I do,' said Harry calmly. She reached for the Path. forms in the rack and filled out a couple, requesting tests for blood and chromosomes. 'I'm a little worried that he's so well developed, and yet he's got this problem with his leg muscles. I think we'll start by doing a couple of tests to see if there's anything we've missed.'

'Do you know what's wrong? Is it serious?' asked the mother.

'I really can't say until we've done the tests,' Harry said guardedly. 'But don't worry too much about it right now. I'd like you to go with the nurse and have some blood taken for these tests. Then perhaps you could come back here because I'd like Matthew to be seen by the paediatric consultant, Dr Buchanan. He's an expert on these things,' she finished, trying to look more positive than she felt.

Mother and son went off down the corridor with the nurse, leaving Harry to steady her nerves. Be calm and professional, she schooled herself, that's all there is to it. 'Is Dr Buchanan still here?' she asked Sister who opened the door of his room to check. He was in there alone, jotting down notes on the patients he'd seen.

'Problems?' He looked up at her and she couldn't fail to notice in his face the grey signs of strain that were so evident in her own. He was wearing a light suit and another of his brilliant ties, and his stethoscope dangled nonchalantly around his neck. She cast her eyes down to the desk, halted by a kick inside, a sudden lurch of pain.

'Just the one. Matthew Mayer, aged thirty-four months, development quite normal until the last few months when he's begun to suffer from weakness in his buttocks and thighs.' She put the child's notes down on the desk. 'It looks to me like a textbook case of Duchennes muscular dystrophy. Everything fits. When he tried to stand up he went straight into the dying gladiator posture. I thought you'd want to take a look.'

'Where is he now?' Tom flipped through the notes, stopping when he came to her neat hand-written observations.

'Gone for tests. I've asked for a chromosome count; if he turns out to be XXY we'll know exactly what we're dealing with,' she said briskly. Duchennes muscular dystrophy was an unpleasant disease usually linked to an extra X chromosome. It led to the gradual wasting of the muscles, first in the legs but later throughout the body, including the heart. Children suffering from the condition usually died young.

'Poor kid. As you say, all the symptoms point in that

direction. Well spotted.' Tom closed the folder and she could feel him looking at her, staring her up and down, his eyes burning holes in the smart coffee-coloured linen suit she was wearing. She turned to go.

'Hold on, he'll be back in five minutes and we can see him together. It'll be much less alarming for his mother.'

Harry gestured to her watch. 'It's getting late and you've got a ward round at two-thirty. If I don't grab some lunch now I'll never get it.'

She made the mistake of glancing back at him and found herself immediately hooked by the intensity of his eyes. 'You haven't been down to the canteen all week. Your absence has been noted and commented on.' His voice was like navy velvet. 'And to be honest, Harry, it's beginning to show.' He stood up and walked to the door, leaning with his back against it and blocking her escape. 'I hate to see you looking like this.' As he said it, he reached out to touch her cheek. Harry leapt backwards across the room like a scalded cat.

'You know the reason better than anyone.' Unconsciously she rubbed her cheek where he had attempted to touch it. 'And I couldn't give a damn for your opinion about the way I look.' Behind her she felt the low barrier of the examination couch. 'Anyway, it's all for my own good, isn't it? Just think of this as my course of chemotherapy; you've introduced a few toxins into my system and they'll give me a month or two of suffering, but once the treatment's over I'll be a new woman. You can discharge me and forget about it. All sorted out, thanks to you.' All the bitterness she'd been storing up came bubbling to the surface, visibly stinging him.

'Is that what you really feel?'

'We agreed not to talk about feelings. From now on it's all strictly business, remember?' Harry toyed with the lamp fixed over the couch, switching it on and off. He ignored her.

'You know, of course, that the treatment doesn't always work,' he said enigmatically. 'Sometimes we have to look for an alternative solution.'

'I assure you that it's working wonders in my case.'

'Then bear in mind that it's sometimes worse for the person standing by, helpless, than it is for the patient undergoing the treatment.'

Harry turned scathing eyes on him, unable to interpret the meaning of his words. Was he saying that he'd hated humiliating her the other evening, when he'd held her naked in his arms, then unceremoniously thrown her out? She gave a hollow laugh. 'Don't tell me that after all you've done I'm supposed to be feeling sorry for *you*?'

'I'm not sure what I want you to feel for me.' He gave her a troubled smile that for a second seemed to stop her heart. Harry waited. All she wanted was a clue, a reason to understand why he had knowingly hurt her, but it was not to be. As she stood there, captured in the burning sapphire of his eyes, there was a knock at the door. Tom turned, shaking his head as if emerging from a dream, and Sister appeared and announced that Mrs Meyer and Matthew were waiting. The instant was over.

His final words stayed with her all afternoon, repeated in her ear like the refrain of some banal pop song that she couldn't get out of her head. As she drove home late that afternoon she found herself wondering yet again what he had meant. There had been no other clues during the meeting with Mrs Mayer. He'd handled that situation beautifully, making it clear that they suspected something was seriously wrong, but not alarming her unduly. When mother and son had left to go home, he'd raced off without another word.

Still musing about it, Harry let herself into the flat. The doormat was littered with envelopes from local estate agents, all with details of flats for sale in the local area. She picked them up and dumped them unopened on the kitchen table. 'Gina?' she opened the boxroom door but there was no one there. Everything looked just as it had this morning. Harry looked around, feeling for the first time a twinge of real concern.

She'd pushed worries about Gina to the back of her mind, half believing that she'd get home this evening and find her sister curled on the sofa watching *Wogan*. But there was still no sign of her. Harry looked round. She'd always prided herself on giving Gina complete privacy and never poked through her belongings, but now, she told her conscience, circumstances were different. What she needed was a clue—anything which might indicate what was wrong, or where Gina had gone. And if there were no clues, the police would have to be alerted. Not that there was anything they could do. Gina was an adult, and adults were allowed to go off and do what they liked—there was no obligation for them to tell anyone where they were going, or when they'd be back.

With that knowledge in mind, Harry started with the dressing table, opening drawers and sorting through the selection of make-up, underwear and sweaters, sifting through the papers and notes Gina had accumulated during her few brief weeks on the typing course. There was nothing much except a dog-eared sheet of paper with a number of names and addresses on it. Harry read them quickly. Paul, the boy with whom Gina had broken up, was listed. She stuffed the paper in her pocket. Quite a few things were missing, she realised, including Gina's diary, and her building society savings book, which was normally lying around.

Guiltily, not really sure what she was looking for, she opened the door of the wardrobe and began to check the pockets of the clothes. There was nothing except a few old bus tickets. Harry reached up to shift some of the shoes and boxes on the shelf above the clothes rail. As she moved a shoebox she heard something rattling inside. Curiously she opened the lid, then sat down quickly on the bed. She'd never had to buy or use a pregnancy testing kit herself, but it didn't take much intelligence for her to work out what the little plastic containers and test tubes were. She sat there in a state of shock for some minutes.

So this was what Gina had been so upset about—she was pregnant. Harry's mind went back to the conversations she'd had with her sister; she could clearly remember a number of moments when Gina had seemed to be summoning up the courage to say something, but had backed down at the last moment. She looked back down at the contents of the box. What an idiot she was not to realise what was going on! How could she have been so short-sighted?

The insistent shrilling of the bleeper in her bag roused her from her thoughts. Harry left the shoebox on the bed and went to the phone. The switchboard put her through to Rupert Ward.

'Sorry to call you out, Harry,' apologised the staff

nurse, 'but we've got a problem with one of your patients, Richard Small, the boy who had his tonsillectomy this afternoon. His pulse rate's up and his blood pressure is slightly down.'

Harry was already reaching for her bag, all thoughts of Gina banished. 'I'm on my way,' she promised. 'Meanwhile, get him sitting up and take his pulse and BP every five minutes. And you'd better get some blood lined up in case we have to transfuse him. I'll be as quick as I can, but if there's anyone available on the premises, alert them.' She was out of the door almost before the receiver was down. From the symptoms she suspected that he was haemorrhaging, and that could be a major problem.

By the time she reached Rupert Ward the curtains had been drawn around the bed and there were signs of activity. Harry slipped through the opening. 'How are we doing?' she asked.

'Very nicely, thank you.' Tom smiled slightly as he looked up from his position by the bedside where he was inserting a cannula into the back of Richard's hand for the blood transfusion. The staff nurse was holding the boy's arm still. Harry watched as Tom found the vein and inserted the needle and cannula. With a few reassuring words to Richard, he removed the needle and clipped the connector in place. It was difficult not to admire the skill with which he worked. No struggling and stabbing, no blood on the sheet, just the gentle but firm pressure of his strong fingers on the child's wrist. He had the authority of long practice; six years ago, when she'd first met him, he'd probably been a houseman like her. Putting up a drip was nothing new to him, though these days, as a consultant, he was rarely required to do so. 'Harry, perhaps you could help with the tape?' His voice was quiet, yet compelling.

She took the roll of plaster from the dressings trolley and cut three lengths, handing them to him one by one so that he could secure the infusion in place. 'Thanks,' he nodded when it was done. He placed the boy's hand flat on the bed and, holding it there, explained why he must keep it still and let the blood drip into the vein. Richard listened, breathing noisily because of his naso-gastric tube, and when his hand was released he obediently left it lying there.

'Good lad.' Without further comment Tom went to wash his hands. Harry, feeling redundant and with the now familiar turmoil of emotions stirring inside her, checked the chart at the end of the bed, and then sat talking to Richard as she took his blood pressure. It was already rising and she filled the new figure in. She was too busy chatting to the boy to notice the curtain open and Tom return to the bedside. The next thing she knew, he'd reached over her shoulder and taken the chart from her. His fingers, cool after being washed in cold water, brushed hers firmly. His touch, she knew, was no accident. Trying to hide her reaction from Richard, Harry smiled, and shifted position away from the man who was standing perilously close behind her—so close she could feel his jacket brushing her shoulders.

There was a metallic clatter as the pen rolled off her lap and on to the floor. She bent swiftly to pick it up, and at precisely the same moment he went to retrieve it. Their foreheads met with a resounding bump and for a second, time seemed to stand still. Harry felt her cheek pressed hard against his, burning at the warmth of him.

Her foot shot from under her as she tried to keep her balance, and for one terrible moment she thought she was going to tip off the bed and into his arms. Then suddenly he caught her, his fingers as firm and strong and gentle as they had been when they held Richard's wrist, and he lifted her back on to the bed.

Despite his sore throat and the tube up his nose, Richard giggled. 'Ouch!' Tom rubbed his temple with an exaggerated wince. He turned to Harry, who was more aware of the burning of her cheeks and her arms where he'd touched her than the bump on her head. 'Sorry about that. Is your forehead sore?'

Before she could answer, he examined her brow, and gently stroked the red mark that was already appearing. 'We were talking about cures this afternoon, weren't we? You know what the best cure for this is, don't you?' he asked.

'An icepack,' Harry said quickly, seeing what was coming, but it was too late to escape. Holding her still, his hands cupping her face, he kissed her forehead gently—like a parent kissing a child better. Richard giggled again. Tom's lips found the sore spot once more, and she thought, or perhaps just imagined, the moist warmth of his tongue tasting her skin.

'Is that better?' He asked it so quietly that she knew it was for her ears only.

Harry swallowed the lump that was threatening to choke her. 'No,' she said feebly, 'you've just made everything much worse.' Swiftly she grabbed the cubicle curtain and swished it back, revealing them to the curious gaze of the rest of the ward. 'I'll stay with Richard for a while,' she announced. 'I'm sorry you were bothered.'

'That's OK. I'm glad to help out.' He walked a few steps from the bed, beckoning her to follow. His blue eyes were glittering with amusement and Harry could feel her heart turning crazy somersaults in her breast. There was something playful about him, something she hadn't seen before. And then suddenly he was being completely professional. 'Richard should be all right now. We aspirated his stomach contents before you arrived and he doesn't appear to have swallowed much blood. He's had some cryopecipitate to help the clotting, so I don't foresee any more problems.'

'I'll hang around for a while, just in case,' Harry insisted.

'Well, if you've nothing better to do . . .' He bowed his head mockingly. Harry watched him leave, noting the spring to his step. Perhaps, she thought, he liked the opportunity to do the kind of hands-on routine jobs normally carried out by housemen. Or perhaps he was just feeling pleased with himself because he had managed to make a fool of her all over again. Cursing him, she went off to the office. She could spend a useful hour typing up letters to be sent to the GPs whose cases she had seen this morning. But it was a waste of time, she realised when she saw the amount of waste paper piling up in the bin. The keys of the typewriter blurred as she looked at them and she made a hundred stupid errors.

She felt the tears beginning to prick her eyes. It was all too much to bear. First Tom and now Gina. Why was she the one who had to be lumbered with all the problems? Just thinking of Tom filled her with a physical ache. What did he want from her? How on earth was she to understand anything when his attitude towards her changed like the wind, one day cold and distant, the next day warm and caring, kissing her as he had this evening . . . as he had on Saturday evening, before he'd suddenly turned on her. Harry rapped her knuckles hard on the desk, trying to distract her thoughts. It didn't work. The pride that had kept her going for the last few days evaporated and she sat hunched over the typewriter, crying uncontrollably.

Her eyes were still red and her cheeks blotchy when she went down to the ward to check on Richard. He was dozing and she could see from his blood pressure and pulse chart that everything was as it should be.

'He can go on to half-hourly observation now,' Harry instructed the night sister, too embarrassed to look the woman in the face. 'Any changes and I want to know about them.' She felt in her pocket for a handkerchief to blow her nose but instead pulled out the sheet of paper she'd found in Gina's room. 'Is there an A-Z guide to London anywhere?' she asked, an idea forming in her mind. She'd go and see Paul now and find out if he knew where Gina was. No matter how shattered she felt, it would be better than going back to the flat and sitting there all night worrying.

There was no London road map to be found. Harry stood looking blankly at the address, her mind numbed by exhaustion and unhappiness. 'He lives in N1. That's Islington, isn't it?' But what was she going to do, she thought despairingly—comb every backstreet and byway until she found the right one?

Night Sister shrugged. 'Maybe Dr Tom can help.' She slipped the paper from Harry's grasp and waved it and, as if from nowhere, Tom materialised at their side. Harry tried to shade her pink-rimmed eyes but knew from his quick glance that he'd noticed she'd been crying. 'Do you know where this address is?'

He studied it silently for a few seconds, then nodded. 'Islington, eh? I used to live there years ago. I think Gerrard Road is up near Camden Passage and all those antique shops. It's not far from the Angel.' Sister held out her hands to Harry in a gesture that said 'problem solved', then hurried off to check on her nurses. Tom turned silently. He seemed bigger, and more brooding than ever. 'Why do you want to go to Islington at this time of night? You'd be better off going straight home to bed.' There was concern in his voice.

Harry tried to snatch the sheet of paper from him but he jerked it out of her reach. Not another argument, not now, she wanted to protest. She simply couldn't face it. 'I just have to go and see someone there, that's all.' Never mind the paper, she could remember the address.

'Harry, you're practically dead on your feet. Surely it's nothing so urgent that it can't wait until you've had a decent night's sleep?'

Harry tried to summon the energy to stand up to him, but it wouldn't come. She was tired and hungry, her body and her brain were feeling more dulled than they ever had before, and she couldn't find a single dreg of indignation to get the sparks going. 'I have to go,' she said simply. 'My sister's disappeared and I need to ask her old boyfriend if he knows where she's gone.'

'And this is his address?' Tom took another look at the paper.

'Why else would I need to know where it was?' Harry tried to step past him but he blocked her. 'I don't want to go, but Gina may be in trouble . . . I think she's pregnant. I need to find her and sort it out.' She looked up at him, unaware that in the brilliant fluorescent lights of the ward the tracks of her tears were clearly visible on her cheeks. 'Please, I'm too tired to argue with you now.'

He hesitated for a long time, studying her face until she could bear his scrutiny no longer and found herself gazing shiftily at the ground. 'I'll take you to Islington. I know it's against our rules—but I've broken them twice today already.' He smiled and she saw once more that flickering glow in his eyes.

Harry felt the tears threatening to fall again. Her mind and body seemed to have developed a life of their own, totally beyond her control. Right now she wasn't even sure she *could* have found her way to Islington, if she'd wanted to. 'Look, this is all my fault. Let me deal with it in my own way.'

'Sure,' he noded. 'I'll drive you there and bring you back. I'm not doing it for any selfish reasons, you understand, I just want to protect the city's pedestrians from being mown down when you fall asleep at the wheel.'

Resignation, heavy as a blanket, and strangely comforting too, descended on Harry's shoulders. It was easier to give in than to protest—easier to be with him than to escape. She sighed. He'd won again, another crushing victory. Against him she was totally powerless. He knew her weaknesses and hit out at them with frightening accuracy. He'd known how she'd dreamed of him, how she'd wanted him, and he'd used her desire as a weapon to hurt her. He'd seen through the pleasant façade of her life with Anthea and Melanie, and unerringly uncovered the truth that she herself had denied. What point was there in trying to stop him now?

He could do with her what he wanted. She shrugged casually, anxious not to appear grateful. 'All right. You can't do any more damage than you've done already. Let's go.'

CHAPTER TEN

HE DROVE like a taxi-driver, taking the back doubles rather than queueing at traffic lights on the main routes through the city. He obviously knew his way around, Harry thought, trying to keep track of where they were. It was dark by the time the car pulled up in Islington. 'That's the house.' He pointed to a white-fronted Georgian place with a red front door and three bell-pushes. 'Do you want me to come with you?'

'No.' She got out, climbed the front steps and rang the bell that was labelled with Paul's surname. There was no answer.

'He's not in, obviously.' Tom had silently joined her. 'What do you want to do? Is there anywhere else we can go to look for your sister?' Harry's hackles rose. So it was 'we' now, was it? Suddenly the search for Gina had become a joint venture.

Before she could protest there was the sound of a key being turned in the lock and a young man whom she vaguely recognised opened the door. He was wearing a towelling bathrobe and his hair was wet. 'Sorry,' he said, 'I was in the shower.' He looked at her curiously. 'You're Gina's sister, aren't you?'

Harry nodded. 'Gina's gone missing and I'm trying to find out where she is. Can I come in for a minute?'

Paul looked past her to the dark figure of Tom. 'I suppose so,' he said, and suddenly she sensed that he was nervous about something. He led them up the stairs to the top floor flat, Harry burningly aware that Tom was following her in. He had no right to intrude like this, she thought, but for some reason she didn't tell him so. Having him there gave her a strange kind of confidence. Paul let them into his sitting-room, which was cheerful and scruffy at the same time—like Gina's room at home. He threw himself on to the old sofa and Harry perched on a dining chair. Tom stood silently by the door, keeping out of the way, but casting a brooding shadow.

'Now, what's this all about?' Paul reached for the packet of cigarettes that was lying on the floor and lit one up. Harry spotted a pair of women's high-heeled shoes protruding from under the sofa. 'I haven't seen Gina for . . .' he paused to think, 'getting on for two weeks. That was when we decided to call it a day.'

'Why?' asked Harry. 'She was very upset about it. I don't think she wanted to break up with you.'

He looked at her strangely, then blew a smoke ring. 'She was getting too serious. I had to make it clear to her that I had no intention of being tied down.'

'Did she tell you she was pregnant?' Harry leaned forward. There was something about him she didn't like—something narcissistic. Paul cast a quick look in Tom's direction.

'She told me she thought she was pregnant and she wanted to know what I was going to do about it.'

'And what did you say?'

He examined his cigarette lighter. 'I told her that she was going to have to work it out on her own. Look,' he shrugged, 'I'm twenty-two and I have no intention of getting tied down with a wife and kid. She knew that.

What we both wanted was a good time—parties, drinking, nightclubs, all that. Not a wedding-ring and nappies.'

Harry could scarcely believe her ears. 'So you just told her to get lost?' Her voice rose in pitch. 'You take no responsibility for it at all?'

He laughed dismissively. 'Look, it was a strictly fun relationship and Gina knew the rules. She told me she was on the Pill and I believed her——'

'And you never let it enter your head that it was anything more serious as far as she was concerned?'

'That was her look-out. I promised her nothing.' He glared at Harry. 'I have no intention of sitting here and letting you moralise at me. Maybe the pair of you are stupid enough to believe in love and marriage and all that rubbish, but reality is different—and kids today know it. This is Thatcher's Britain; decide what you want and get out there and grab it, that's the message.'

Harry shook her head in disbelief, the coals of her anger beginning to smoulder. 'I've never heard such arrogant, selfish garbage in my life!' She stood up, leaning over him as he reclined on the sofa. 'How could you be so bloody irresponsible? You talk of having a fun relationship, when really you mean that you just want to do what you like—have a good time, and the minute anyone disagrees with you, ditch them. You didn't care anything about her at all, did you, yet you strung her along——'

'You're so old-fashioned!' He gave her a patronising smile, but behind it Harry saw the flicker of self-doubt. He was putting on a big act, she felt sure. No one could be this callous. 'It's not like that at all. We're out of the Dark Ages now and women are responsible for themselves. I'm sorry if Gina's run away and I'm sorry if she's pregnant and you're going to have to sort it out, but that's the way things are. *C'est la vie.*'

'What if something dreadful happens to her? What if she tries to do something stupid?'

He took a long drag on the cigarette, then stubbed it out firmly in the saucer by his side. It was supposed to be a defiant gesture but Harry noticed that the pulse in his throat was beating hard and fast and his palms were shiny with sweat. The veneer of his devil-may-care attitude was wearing thin. 'Look, she's quite old enough to take care of herself. I feel no guilt or responsibility towards her whatsoever. Gina's not going to chuck herself in the Thames just because she's pregnant. Anyway,' he added darkly, 'she's probably gone away for a couple of days to get that dealt with. You're a doctor, you know about these things.' For a second he hesitated, then added with bravado, 'I wouldn't mind seeing her again once she's got it all fixed. She's a nice girl.'

Harry exploded. If she'd been a man she would have thrown a punch. As it was, she grabbed the nearest thing to hand, which happened to be a cup of cold coffee, and threw that instead. He fended it off with his arm but the mug smashed against the wall and coffee splattered everywhere. 'You're the lousiest, dirtiest creep I've ever had the misfortune to meet!' Inarticulate with fury, she kicked him hard in the shin. 'I thought I'd met some pretty nasty, calculating specimens but you're the very worst. What on earth did Gina see in you? You're such a stupid, immature, pathetic excuse for a man! I'm stunned that she couldn't find anyone better.' Her stabbing finger emphasising every word,

Harry leaned over him. 'If anything happens to her, you're the one who's responsible. Do you understand me? You can't just do what you like to people, then wash your hands of it and stroll away. That's a lesson you're going to have to learn the hard way.' Clenching her hands, she swung round looking for the way out. In the heat of the moment she'd forgotten Tom. Now he stepped back and she marched straight from the room.

Behind her she heard his gravelly voice say quietly, 'We can let ourselves out.' He followed her down the stairs, opened the car door for her, then got in himself, but he didn't switch the engine on. Harry sat in the passenger seat, pounding her knees with her bunched fists, tears of frustration and exhaustion stinging her eyes.

'God, what a bastard! I'd like to strangle him.' Tom was silent. She was so wrapped up in her own feelings that she wasn't aware of the shaken look on his face, or the way he was watching her. Harry began to tremble, just slightly at first, then violently, until it wasn't just her hands but her whole body that was quaking. 'This is ridiculous,' she said, trying to sound amused at her body's reaction. Holding out one wrist she watched her fingers shuddering. 'What's happening to me?'

Tom took her hand, his fingers seeking her pulse. 'You're freezing.' He was absolutely calm. Reaching round to the back seat, he found a Barbour jacket of waxed green cotton and arranged it round her, tucking it well in. 'There's only so much a body can put up with—as you should know, Dr Hart.' He spoke with utter professionalism, no joking, no sarcasm. Harry felt as Richard Small must have felt earlier in the evening as Tom had worked methodically on him—uncomfortable, but trusting, aware of his gentle authority and unquestioning of it. 'You're tired and I doubt whether you've bothered to eat anything all day. You're under stress at home and work. Is it any wonder that your body is trying to tell you something?'

As he spoke, the jacket fell off her left shoulder. Harry tried to pick it up but he brushed her hand away. She turned to look at him and found his face just inches from her own. His expression troubled her; there was a streak of raw pain in his eyes. And then it faded.

'Come here,' he said, and his voice was so tender that it melted her heart. His arms encompassed her, crushing her to his chest. Harry just lay there against him, too shattered to analyse what was going on, too confused even to think, just grateful to share the warmth of his body. 'Everything's going to be all right.' He murmured it so softly into her ear that she might have imagined it, but it touched something deep within her. She felt a sudden, unstoppable flood of relief—totally irrational and overwhelming. It was as if, all her life, she'd been waiting to hear those words; as if, secretly, she'd schooled herself never to expect them. She began to cry, loud, racking sobs that tore through her body until all that she was aware of were his arms clutching her tightly against him and the sound of his voice whispering her name over and over again.

It seemed to last an age, but eventually the final sob subsided. Harry felt suddenly self-conscious and drew away, wiping her eyes on the backs of her hands, searching for her handbag in which there was a wad of tissues. Silently he took the handkerchief from his breast pocket and, like a mother wiping a small child's grimy face, began to dry her cheeks and eyes. Then he gave it to her and she blew her nose noisily. When at last she felt that her vocal cords might be working again, she said embarrassedly, 'I'm sorry. I'm not normally like this.'

He smoothed the damp hair back from her forehead. 'Don't you think I know that?' The car ignition was so quiet that Harry barely noticed he'd switched the engine on. 'There's nothing more we can do about Gina tonight. I'm taking you home.'

Harry said nothing. She felt drained of every last ounce of strength and emotion. She couldn't have done anything more tonight if she'd wanted to. They had just passed King's Cross when she fell asleep, and she was still asleep when the car pulled up. She was dimly aware of the door opening and closing, of footsteps on the pavement and the jangling of door keys, but she couldn't rouse herself. Just let her sleep here, warm and comfortable, that was all she wanted.

Her door opened and the cool evening air fanned round her legs. Tom leaned over and unclipped her seatbelt, then put his arm behind her shoulders. 'Come on, you can't spend the night in here.' Gently he levered her out, still half wrapped in his jacket. For the first time, Harry opened her eyes. It was an effort.

'This isn't my house.' They were in Campden Hill Square. Light from his hall flooded on to the pavement through the open front door.

'No,' he said calmly, 'it's mine. You can stay here for tonight. I don't think it's a good idea for you to be alone.'

'And *I* don't think it's a good idea for me to stay here.' Harry stood, swaying slightly, on the pavement. Suddenly her mind seemed clear, unclouded by all the doubts and emotions that had made her so confused. It was as if her confrontation with Paul, and her tears, had driven all that away.

'Why?' His blue eyes searched hers.

Harry felt a laugh rising in her throat, but as it reached her mouth it turned into a sob. She shook her head. What good would she do by telling him? But why not be honest? Why torture herself with it when it was easier to tell him? 'I've fallen in love with you.'

What had she expected him to do? Laugh? Tell her not to be so stupid? Instead he seemed to do nothing. There was the merest flicker of light in his eyes, the slightest shadow of a smile across his mouth. Then he sighed and brushed his fingers lightly across her cheek. 'All the more reason for you to come in, then.' She half expected, half wanted him to kiss her, but he didn't. Obediently she followed him into the house.

'What you need is a night's undisturbed sleep. The bedroom's up there on the right. There's a bathroom off it. Have a bath if you want. I'll get you something to eat.' He turned back quickly. 'Leave your bleep down here in the hall. If you're called out, I'll go into St Hugh's. That way you can get some rest.'

Harry paused at the bottom of the stairs, shaming memories of her last visit returning. 'There's no need for that. I'm on call so I should be the one to go.' The banisters seemed to be swaying in front of her eyes. She lurched forward and tripped up the first step.

Tom caught her before she did any serious damage to herself, or the fabric of the house. 'You're in no fit state to go anywhere,' he muttered, scooping her up into his arms. 'You're asleep on your feet.'

Harry didn't argue. She could barely keep her eyes

open; already she could feel herself drifting off in her arms, and even the sensation of his hand gripping her bare thigh wasn't enough to rouse her from her torpor. She nestled her head against his shoulder, feeling like one of the sleepy children on the ward who dozed off trustingly on a nurse's lap. She was too tired to worry what he'd think, too tired to want to know how he was feeling, too tired to care about anything in the world. He could put her down wherever he wanted—in his bed, in the bath, on the bare boards of the landing—and she would just curl up and sleep.

He kicked open the bedroom door with his foot and carried her in, placing her carefully on one side of the bed. She rolled over, trapping his hand underneath her leg. Tom extricated it carefully, his fingers stroking the soft, secret skin of her thigh, teasing the tendons at the back of her knee. He eased off her shoes, then lifted her shoulders as he tried to pull off her linen jacket, which was beginning to resemble a crumpled rag. His hand caught her breast and lingered and he heard her give a low moan in her sleep. Tentatively he touched her again, feeling the firmness of her flesh, the nipple hardening responsively under the thin fabric of her blouse and bra. She sighed and opened her eyes slightly and he pulled away, frightened of waking her, frightened of losing his self-control and, above all, frightened of saying things to her now, in this state, which she'd never remember in the morning. He pulled the bedspread up and over her, wrapping her in its quilted layers, and then, satisfied that she would be warm enough, tore himself away from temptation.

Hours later, Harry stirred in her warm cocoon. She'd been dreaming that someone was watching her; that a pair of aquamarine eyes were focused on her, silently observing her every move. She lay still for a moment, swallowing, trying to work out where she was and why she seemed to be wrapped in a blanket, instead of her usual duvet. Memory returned hazily. She looked towards the window where the moonlight was streaming in, and found Tom standing over her, silently watching, just like the watcher in her dream. For a long, long time he just gazed at her, his face shadowed except for the blue gleam in his eyes, and then she blinked—and when she looked again he was gone, leaving her wondering if she was still dreaming, and not caring if she was or not.

It was the sun that woke her the second time. It was dancing in patterns over the bed, dappled by the leaves of the tree outside the window. Harry rolled over, burying her face in the pillow and breathing in the unmistakable scent of the man she'd just dreamt of, faint but powerful on the pillowslip. So, she thought slowly, this was his bed, and he slept on this side of it. But he hadn't been here last night. He hadn't wanted to share it with her. The old ache, the one she thought she'd exorcised last night, returned with its dull, familiar rhythm. Harry's eyes roved round the room, taking in the ornate plaster coving and the majestic ceiling rose. The windows were huge and looked out over an overgrown garden in which the statue of a faun stood forlornly on a plinth. Like the other rooms of the house she'd seen, this one was bare and undecorated, its walls stripped of the old paper, the boards uncovered except for the Turkish carpet on which the bed stood. She sat up, stretching her arms out of the quilt, yawning widely . . .

And then she saw it, staring down at her from the wall opposite the bed. Her portrait—the portrait Anthea had painted of her. Harry felt her heart stop as she surveyed it. The slight smile, the air of exasperation, the distance and defensiveness in the cool green eyes. And she realised with another twinge of pain that Anthea had got it right; Anthea knew her better than she did herself. Anthea and Tom—they'd instinctively known the things that she'd hidden from herself. Perhaps that was why they'd both hit it off so well together. She sat hugging her knees, studying it again.

When she'd seen the picture the first time it had bothered her; she'd felt there was something worrying about it. Now she knew the truth about herself, she could look at it and like what she saw. Maybe it didn't portray the innocent, sweet-faced girl she'd imagined herself to be—but now she knew she wasn't like that, anyway. That was the only good thing to come out of this horrible mess. Her innocence had been shattered and painfully replaced by self-knowledge; Tom had woken in her all kinds of emotions and feelings that she'd been holding at bay for too long. It hurt but it was for the best. If she could just survive this difficult patch, everything would be all right.

Harry slipped out of her makeshift sleeping bag and crossed the floor to the fireplace, where her shoes and jacket had been neatly arranged on a chair. With them was a note written in Tom's strong, untidy black hand, informing her that there was no need for her to go into St Hugh's until lunchtime, reminding her to have a decent breakfast, and warning her that the builders might be arriving to work on the top floor of the house. Nothing about last night, she noted. He'd carefully evaded all mention of that. At the bottom of the note was scrawled the telephone number of the local cab company, to take her home. He thought of everything, Harry smiled. How nice to have someone sorting things out for her, instead of having to fix everything for others.

He'd also left her two individual keys, one for the deadlock on the way out, as he instructed in his note, and a Yale for getting back in. Harry weighed the second key in her hand, trying to gauge what he'd meant by leaving it for her. She didn't need it—she had no reason to come back, had she? Confused by it all, she went to wash her face in the bathroom.

It felt strangely intimate to be here when he wasn't around. She considered having a bath, but the threat of the builders arriving put her off and, anyway, she had nothing clean to change into. She found herself examining the various bottles and soaps ranged along the shelves, but like the rest of the house they seemed to offer just a vague and tantalising glimpse of their owner. Harry fought back against the desire to look through his wardrobe and riffle through the chest of drawers, as she had done yesterday in Gina's room. She checked herself in the huge mirror behind the door and found herself imagining Tom's reflection in it as he stepped naked out of the bath. The thought was enough to freeze her. She stood rooted to the spot, seeing him as if he was really there, while all the time the intense pain of her wanting, and the knowledge that she could never have him, battled in her stomach. When the pain got too much to bear she ran her comb quickly through her hair and raced down the stairs.

Although it was only nine-thirty the cab company was already busy. They warned her she'd have to wait twenty minutes for a car and she spent the time unashamedly exploring. The rooms were huge and elegant, all of them stripped and ready for redecorating. The kitchen had been gutted, but the process of redecoration had already begun and new units built of bleached oak were being constructed and fitted. In what she presumed was the utility room she found a kettle, a fridge and a microwave. Above them, neatly arranged, were coffee, breakfast cereal, eggs and cans of tuna—the kind of staples kept by anyone forced to live without a kitchen.

If the taxi hadn't arrived she might have spent the morning there. As it was, she was soon back in her own, much less grand flat. She went first into the bathroom to run a bath, then into a kitchen to put on the kettle for coffee. She was just about to go back to the bathroom when she noticed that the estate agents' envelopes, which she'd flung on the table when she'd got in yesterday evening, had been opened and the descriptions of the various places for sale spread out. The hair on the back of her neck seemed to stand on end. Who could have got in? Anthea was the only one to have a key—and Gina.

A noise behind her made her whirl round. Gina stood there, pale and worried-looking, dressed in frayed jeans. 'Where on earth have you been?' Harry raced across the room to her sister and flung her arms around her neck. 'I've been worried sick about you. I went to see Paul last night to see if he knew where you'd gone.' She was surprised at her own strength of emotion. There had been times when she'd thought she'd be glad if she never saw Gina again.

Gina was crying, hugging her back. 'What did he say?'

Harry held her sister at arm's length. 'He wasn't very nice. I'm sorry, but he didn't seem very concerned about you. The only person he really cares for is himself.'

Gina wiped her eyes. 'I know. I thought he'd help, but he turned out to be . . . well, he wasn't what I thought he was. Did he tell you about . . .' she faltered and blushed.

'About you being pregnant?' Harry hugged her again. 'Yes, he did.' She hesitated. 'He seemed to think you'd run off to have the baby aborted.'

'That was the general idea.' Gina detached herself from Harry's grip, calmer now. 'I couldn't go and see any doctors around here in case you knew them, and I didn't dare go home to see Dr Talbot. He would have phoned Mum straight away and told her——'

'No, he wouldn't,' inserted Harry. 'He's bound by the same rules of confidentiality as we all are, whether he likes it or not.'

'Well, I didn't want to see him. I've been going to him since I was a kid. He's like a friend of the family. So I went down to Southampton to stay with Lizzie—you know, the girl I used to go to school with.'

Harry nodded and began to make coffee. 'Why didn't you tell me? About Paul and going to Lizzie's and the baby and everything? Honestly, Gina, I know I nag you from time to time, but you can trust me. I've spent the last twenty-four hours worried that you were going to be discovered dead in a ditch somewhere.'

Gina had the grace to look ashamed of herself. 'I just phoned Lizzie out of the blue and she said I could go down there, so I did. I tried to tell you, Harry, but it wasn't easy—and then you were moping around after this trouble with Anthea and the new doctor on Paddington, and I knew you'd go berserk if I told you—so I just grabbed my things and went.'

'And?' Harry asked. 'What's the situation?' Years of working in hospitals had made her quite matter-of-fact about such things.

'I'm not pregnant.'

'You *were* pregnant and now you're not, or——'

Gina shook her head, 'No, it was a false alarm. I tried one of those kits but it was too early to tell. I was going to go and see Lizzie's doctor and get a proper test, but I didn't need to. Suddenly——' She looked at Harry. 'Look, you're a doctor, I don't have to explain how I knew for sure that I wasn't pregnant, do I?'

Harry grimaced. 'No, they covered that one in medical school. Well, that's a relief. It's a horrible situation to be in—a terrible decision to have to make.'

Gina shuddered. 'Don't talk about it any more. This last week has been hell. I tell you, Harry, I'm not letting it happen again. I've grown up a lot.'

Harry smiled, and found her mouth widening into an uncontrollable grin. 'So have I,' she laughed, shaking her head. 'You would have thought at my age I'd have sorted it all out. I wander round that ward sticking needles in kids, prescribing pills, giving orders to people twice my age, telling parents everything will be all right—and all the time I've been trying to hide the fact that I'm not much more than a kid myself.' Gina looked at her quizzically, not understanding all she meant, but she smiled all the same.

'Men! They're awful, aren't they,' she said, sipping her coffee.

'Some of them are,' Harry agreed. 'And some of

them are just impossible to understand.' They both laughed. Harry looked at her sister thoughtfully. 'I hope this doesn't sound too harsh, but in a way I'm glad it happened—your bust-up with Paul and everything. I haven't been able to talk to you like this for ages.'

Gina shuffled her feet self-consciously. 'I know what you mean. Sometimes when you're in big trouble you find out who your real friends are.'

How true that was, Harry thought. Sometimes your worst enemies turned out to be your best friends. For some reason a slogan that she'd seen written on posters in her student days came floating dimly back from the deep recesses of her memory: 'Today is the first day of the rest of your life'. She looked out of the window, where the brilliant morning sun was beginning to bathe the basement area. She didn't understand why, but she knew instinctively that today was a new beginning for her.

'Help,' she murmured, glancing at the clock, 'I've got to have a bath and get ready. I'm doing a magic show this afternoon.'

Gina shook her head disbelievingly. 'I know the old magic sweets trick, but surely you can't make a whole show out of that?'

'No, but I've been swotting up,' Harry said, gulping down her coffee and feeling light-hearted for the first time in weeks. 'Steve taught me two card tricks and one of the porters showed me how to do the old three cups and a ball thing. And for my *pièce de résistance* I'm going to pull Damian Potter's rabbit out of a hat, and give him a terrific surprise.'

Gina raised her hands. 'I hope the rabbit doesn't give *you* a nasty surprise! I think you're all mad on

Paddington Ward.'

Harry bit her lip. 'No, it's one of the sanest places on earth.'

An hour later, as she climbed the basement steps, she bumped into Anthea, who was lugging a huge portfolio out to the car. They'd exchanged only a few terse words since the scene with Tom. Harry had been too upset and embarrassed to say more. Now she felt a new strength. It was if seeing that portrait of herself again, and recognising herself for what she was, had given her confidence. Anthea smiled gingerly at her. 'How are you?'

'I'm much better.' Harry lifted one end of the portfolio into the back of the Volvo. 'Anthea, I want to say sorry for behaving so badly the other day. Everything you said was true.' Gina's words came to her mind. 'Only a real friend would have been prepared to say all those things to me.'

Anthea pulled a pained face. 'Oh, Harry, you wouldn't believe how bad I've felt about it. And Tom, too. He was so guilty about having come along and stirred things up.'

Harry pretended not to hear, but the words pierced her all the same. So he felt guilty, did he? Perhaps that was why he'd been so protective yesterday. Not because he felt anything for her, but because he thought he owed her something. 'It needed doing,' she said simply. 'All my motives were confused. Anyway, I've been thinking, and I've made a decision to move. I'm very fond of you and Melanie . . .'

'But the time has come for a parting of the ways,' Anthea finished. 'I understand, Harry, and I think it's a good idea. You've been tied to us for too long and it's time you got away. Just don't go too far.'

Harry managed a weak smile. 'Oh, I wasn't thinking of going far.'

'How about Campden Hill Square?' There was a twinkle in Anthea's eye but Harry didn't spot it.

'I couldn't possibly afford it—you have to be seriously rich to live there,' she blurted.

'I wasn't suggesting you buy a place there. I thought perhaps——' Anthea came to a grinding halt. 'It's just that Tom insisted on buying my portrait of you and I thought——'

Harry stepped in quickly. 'As you said just now, he's feeling a bit guilty. That's all there is to it—that and the fact that your paintings are appreciating in value every day. It's probably worth ten times what he paid you for it.' She forced a laugh. 'Anyway, I thought you ought to know that I'm looking for somewhere else. I'll still be available to keep an eye on Melanie if you need me—but she's growing up so fast that she can take care of herself now.'

Anthea nodded. 'It's sometimes difficult to believe, isn't it? Well, Harry, if you're happy then I'm happy too. It's sad in a way, isn't it—like the end of an era. But there's always sometimes new and exciting to look forward to around the corner.'

'Anthea Robson—painter and homespun philosopher!' Harry's smile was genuine this time. They parted with a friendly hug.

Everything seemed to be coming together, Harry thought as she walked down the road. It was like the end of some complicated Shakespearian play in which, during the final act, all the quarrels were resolved, brothers reunited, wrongs righted and happy endings dealt out all round. Well, not quite like that, she corrected herself. Happy endings were too much to expect. But at least she'd be parting amicably from the Robsons. And at least Gina was safe and sound, and infinitely wiser for the shock she'd had. And *she* had the job she'd wanted. Now all she needed to make her life content was to find some way of making her peace with Tom Buchanan. And that was going to be the biggest challenge of all.

CHAPTER ELEVEN

THE rabbit was sitting in a large cardboard box on Pat O'Brien's desk when Harry arrived. She peered in. 'My goodness, it's a monster! I'll never get it in the top hat!'

'It's difficult to believe that Damian was running away from hospital to see that, isn't it?' Pat agreed. 'But Mrs Potter's certain. One look at a snapshot of it, and Damian's eyes lit up, apparently.'

'When they're away from home, kids suddenly develop attachments to all sorts of things. Poor Damian just wants to be at home, and he's pinned his unhappiness on Thumper here.' Harry stroked the rabbit. 'You know, instead of pulling it out of a hat I shall have to heave it out of a cardboard box. I was expecting something smaller, and easier to handle.' She had to suspend her plans at that moment because she was summoned to see a new admission on Teddy Ward. By the time she got back the party was in full swing. It was Patrick's birthday, and all those children who were well enough to enjoy the shenanigans had been grouped round a couple of beds at the end of the ward. There had already been games and presents, and when Harry returned they were well into the cake and cola. Lots of parents had joined their children and it was all great fun. Harry, jogging a child on her knee, joined in the silliness.

When the plates and cake crumbs had disappeared,

and the proceedings had been interrupted to allow routine blood pressure and temperature checks to be made on those who required them, Harry stood up and announced that they were going to put on a show.

'Our first entertainer used to be a stand-up comedian until he broke his leg, so now he's a lie-down comedian—a big hand, please, for Antony!' Antony, still on his back with his leg in traction, told a string of jokes that started harmlessly enough but soon became a shade of pale blue. Harry briskly shut him up before the little ones began asking awkward questions. Sara Talbot was next on the running order, singing a song about a red bus. Then they switched on the tape machine and danced the hokey-cokey. Harry, bent almost double and trying not to giggle too much, shook her own arms and legs about and helped one of the children on crutches to do likewise. 'Oooooh, the hokey-cokey,' everyone chorused enthusiastically—even those who were confined to bed and couldn't dance.

Laughing, her cheeks pink with exertion, Harry looked up to see how the others were doing and met Tom's amused blue gaze. He was holding one of the toddlers in his arms and jiggling her about to the music. Normally, when she looked at him like that, Harry felt a little stab of pain or alarm. But today things were different—or she was different. She smiled back at him, just as she would at any member of staff, and he raised his eyebrows slightly in acknowledgement. Then she turned her attention back to the kids.

The hokey-cokey came to a hysterical end, with most of the participants throwing themselves on to the floor in a big heap. When everyone had been extricated one of the nurses wheeled on a trolley which had been covered for the occasion in a sterile drape, to which half-a-dozen silver stars, made from sweet papers, had been stapled. 'And now,' said Harry, 'for some magic.'

She started with the find-the-lady trick, using a ping-pong ball and three cups, which the porter had taught her. She switched the ball around under the cups, challenging the children to find it. At first everyone was very blasé about it, but when, after a few attempts, they still hadn't got it right, they became fascinated. The boys sat concentrating hard in the front row, watching her hands but unable to see how she was doing it.

Her next trick was based on something she'd seen on TV. She put a chair out and asked for a volunteer. Patrick came forward and sat down. Harry took a box of tissues, pulled one out, crumpled it into a ball in her hand, showed it to him and then, with a cry of 'Abracadabra!', flicked her wrist and sent the tissue flying over his head. 'Look, it's disappeared.' She showed her empty hand to Patrick, who hadn't seen what had happened. Everyone else laughed; they'd seen exactly what was going on. Harry did it again, telling Patrick to watch very closely. Again, one moment the ball was there and the next minute it had gone. He shook his head, mystified, as his friends rolled around laughing. Tom was laughing too. Harry didn't dare look at him but she could hear his distinctively deep tones. Having done the tissue trick a few more times, she put Patrick out of his misery by revealing how it was done and allowing him to try it on another child. There was a round of applause.

'And now,' said Harry, deciding to leave out the card tricks which would be too clever for the little children, 'some magic sweets.' She called the kids out one by one, magicking a sweet or a small toy from their ears, their toes, even from down their sweaters or up their trouser legs. 'And now it's time for the final trick.' She went to the trolley and from the shelf pulled out a cardboard box. 'This box is completely empty.' She allowed it to be passed round. Small fingers were poked in every corner and each centimetre examined before her audience was satisfied that it really was just an empty cardboard box. Harry took it back and stood behind the trolley. 'I'm now going to cover it with this magic cloth.' She tried to pick up the star-spangled cloth but pretended that it was stuck. With the children distracted, for a moment she put the empty box back on the trolley shelf and pulled out the much heavier one with the rabbit in it. Without too much trouble she managed to swap them over, so that the rabbit was now covered with the cloth. For a couple of minutes she kept the audience busy saying a magic spell. Then she lifted the box, cloth and all, and placed it on the chair Patrick had vacated.

'Abracadabra!' they all yelled and she whipped back the cover. 'It's a rabbit,' they shrieked.

'It's *my* rabbit!' came Damian Potter's voice, as he gathered the placid creature in his arms. 'She's magicked Thumper!'

'Excuse me,' Antony's voice cut clearly through the commotion, 'but you're going to have to rethink this trick, Harry. I can see the empty box still on the trolley.' Harry turned and looked. He was right.

She shook her head in mock exasperation. 'Blast! And I thought I'd worked it out perfectly.' The rabbit had grabbed everyone's attention. Almost every child

on the ward was gathered round it, trying to stroke and
cuddle it while Damian told them its name and life
history. Tom was leaning over so that the child in his
arms could have a good view of the magic bunny.
Pleased with herself, Harry trundled the trolley back to
the prep room and disposed of the box and the star-
spangled drape. She thought of going back to join the
party, but there was too much work waiting to be done.
She headed for the office instead.

Half-way down the corridor she heard footsteps
behind her. Footsteps she'd know anywhere. Harry
continued unhurriedly, feeling for the first time a sense
of control over the situation. She wasn't frightened by
him any more. There was nothing to hide and no
dishonesty between them. Whatever he had to say to
her, she was prepared for it. She unlocked the office
door and went in, and a few seconds later he knocked.

'Come in.' He found her sitting on Steve's desk, her
feet balanced on the chair, calm, composed and waiting
for him. He edged in, round the sports bags and coat
stand and the battered desks. Harry smiled and found
she didn't have to force it. 'I'm sorry about the state of
the place. Steve and I spend so much time here it's like a
home from home.'

He cleared a soft drink carton and an old copy of the
Guardian from the top of the low filing cabinet and sat
down opposite her, putting his feet up on the same
chair. They were both at the same height, eye to eye.
Instead of flinching from his look, as she normally did,
Harry held her chin high and returned his gaze. 'I came
to congratulate you on your magic act,' he started
tentatively, as if it wasn't really what he wanted to say
at all. 'The rabbit was such a success that no one

remembered to thank you.'

Harry shrugged. 'It was just a bit of fun. But I should be saying thank you for last night.' She took a deep, calming breath and looked straight at him. 'I was in a terrible state. It was very kind of you to look after me like that. I'm sorry I made such a fool of myself.'

'There's nothing to apologise for, and you know it.' He gave a stifled laugh, turning to look out of the window. 'What an incredible mess we've got ourselves into. I can't think where to begin sorting it out.' Harry waited. Before, she'd always jumped into arguments and precipitated them towards disaster. For once she'd sit quietly and listen.

Tom turned back to her. 'Have you heard anything more about Gina?' Despite her resolution, Harry's heart fell. So he'd come just to find out about Gina.

'Yes,' she said flatly. 'When I got home she was there. It all turns out to have been a false alarm—though the fright's done her good. I'm afraid last night was a wild-goose chase.' She felt quickly in her pocket and found his keys. 'Let me give these back to you while I remember.' She held them out to him.

'I don't want them.' His hands remained firmly on his knees. 'Keep them. I want you to be able to come and go as you please.'

Harry was confused. 'I don't understand.'

'I don't know how to put it any better.' The intensity in his eyes shook her. 'I'll try to explain. Ever since we met, I've been piling the pressure on you. Even that first time, after Alex's crash, I just blundered in and lost my temper—as you did last night. Seeing you lay into Paul was a shock. It made me realise the kind of effect

I must have had on you.'

'There was a difference, though,' Harry interrupted quickly. 'I wasn't responsible for what happened to Alex, but he was responsible for Gina.'

'And I've felt responsible for you.' He sighed. 'You were honest with me last night, so I'll be honest with you. For the past six years or however long it is, I'd been hoping to bump into you one day so that I could apologise, and tell you how unjust I was that night. And when I did finally meet you I realised that it wasn't enough to simply apologise. I thought perhaps you'd have forgotten about the whole incident, but it soon became clear that the things I'd said that night had had a drastic effect on you. You were living under the shadow of the things I'd said—with the guilt that I'd imposed on you.' He ran his hand through his hair and cast her a troubled smile. 'My God, this is beginning to sound like a visit to the consultant psychiatrist, isn't it?'

Harry said nothing. He felt responsibility and guilt towards her; what more could she expect of him? Love? That would be asking for too much. Her silence forced him to go on. 'So I decided that the least I could do was shake you out of this way of thinking—show you that you didn't have to bear the responsibility of Melanie for the rest of your life. I wanted you to see that you have a responsibility to yourself, to be happy.' He traced out the pattern of the woodgrain on the back of the chair. 'Can you understand?'

Harry nodded. 'Yes, yes, I do. It's taken some time, and I hated you for doing it, but I'm getting to the stage now where I can see how I was fooling myself. Such a neat, tidy, sterile life. Well, it hasn't been so neat and tidy the last few days, has it? I suppose I should really

be thanking you for ruining it all.' She didn't wait for a
response. 'Anyway, things are going to change. I saw
Anthea at lunchtime and told her I'm moving. That's
the first step. And from there, who knows?' There was
false brightness in her tone. 'A new job and a new life, I
suppose.'

His finger stopped tracing the smooth pattern of the
wood. 'Is that what you really want?' Harry shrugged
non-committally. Yes, she wanted to get away so that
she could escape the torture of being near him. And no,
the idea of not seeing him was unbearable. 'Last night
when you told me . . .' He looked up at her and she saw
doubt lurking in his eyes.

'I told you I loved you,' she said, and there was a
brittleness in her voice. 'Don't be too alarmed, it's all
part of the new Harry Hart, taking risks, owning up to
her feelings—prepared to get hurt.'

'And you meant it?'

She took a breath. 'Yes, of course I did. I wouldn't
have laid myself on the line if I didn't.'

'And how would you feel if I told you I felt the same
way?' Harry looked at him and there was nothing in his
face to indicate his feelings. Was he playing more
games? Was this another element of the cure he'd
prescribed for her?

'I'd like to believe it,' she said with painful honesty,
'but I can't. I wanted to show you that I loved you that
night after the party and you just threw me out.'

'Because I began to understand how much I really
cared about you.' He smiled and Harry felt her heart
starting to hammer. 'If I'd cared nothing about you I
would have slept with you and that would have been
that—like Paul and his attitude to Gina. But because I

cared for you, I suddenly saw that it had to stop.'

'I thought you didn't want me. I thought you'd just had a sudden attack of guilty conscience.'

He reached for her hand and kissed the palm gently. 'Yes, I felt guilty. I had no idea how you really felt about me. I didn't think it was possible for you to love me after all the things I'd done. All I knew was that I didn't want to take you if you were just turning to me in distress because of my bullying. When we make love I want you to understand how much it means to me.

'I want you on equal terms, Harry. I want you to know exactly how I feel about you. I don't want you to come to me because I've pressured you into it—and I don't want your surrender.' He paused, searching for the words. 'The cure's over. You're your own woman now, free to do whatever you want with your life. And if you want to come to me voluntarily, knowing how I feel about you, I'll do whatever I can to make you happy. That's what the keys to the house are for. I want you to know that you have free access to my life. There's going to be no more force. It's your turn now to decide what you want to do.'

Harry looked at the two keys on the desk. 'Is that it? Access to your house—and your bed? Nothing more?' She thought of that wide white bed with its old quilt. Was there anything more that she could possibly want?

'You've got my love. If you want it.' He leaned over the chair rail and kissed her softly, with the special tenderness she'd felt last night.

'I accept it.' She was surprised by the firmness of her own voice.

'And despite what I said the other night, Harry, you can trust me.' She remembered his reaction when she'd driven off in such a state after her encounter with Anthea. She remembered his gentleness last night, wrapping her up like a child in a blanket. She remembered how good it felt to place her trust in him and be rewarded.

'I already do. Don't you realise that?' She pulled away, a bittersweet smile on her lips. 'Hold on a minute, though. I don't think I like this. You say you want an equal partnership, yet you're just handing all the responsibility over to me. Now I've got to make all the running. I've got to come to you if I want you.'

'I'll carry you off and make mad passionate love to you if that's what you want.' The light was burning fiercely in his eyes. 'I assure you that would be no problem at all. And on the other hand, if you want to spend a few weeks or months finding out more about me, I'll understand.'

'I already know all I need to know about you,' Harry murmured. He kissed her again, so gently, and with so much love, that she thought her heart was going to break with happiness. 'There's just one more thing about this equal opportunities set-up.' Harry eyed him speculatively, seeing his face as it had been shadowed by the moonlight when he'd watched over her last night. 'What if I can't think of anything I'd like more than to live with you for the rest of my life? Do I have to get down on one knee and propose?'

'Seriously?'

She looked at him gravely. 'I wouldn't suggest it unless I was serious.'

'In that case we have to resort to magic.' His eyes were as blue as the Aegean—and just as deep and mysterious to Harry, who couldn't make out whether he was joking or not.

'I hope it works better than my trick with the rabbit,' she commented drily. 'Antony saw right through that.'

'Well . . .' He touched her cheek, looking surprised. 'What's this?'

'Where?' Harry raised her hand to her ear. 'What is it? I'm not coming out in spots, am I? We've got that new kid with measles.' He held out something in front of her, something which appeared to have materialised from her ear.

'Where did you learn to do that?' she asked incredulously, scarcely looking at the ring that lay in his palm.

'I went to the same medical school as you did. We probably learned it from the same professor.' He was suddenly quiet. 'This is what I want to give you. It's just a token, a way of trying to show you how much I love you.'

Harry looked down at the ring in her hand. It was exquisite and obviously antique, fashioned from old gold wrought into a lovers' knot. He slipped it gently on to her finger and it fitted as if it had been made for her. It was so beautiful that Harry wanted to cry. 'I don't have anything to give you,' she said softly. 'Only myself.'

He took her in his arms, and it was like coming home—like infinite love and care and happiness. His voice was just a whisper, but it said all she needed to hear. 'There's nothing in the world I want more.'

Hello!

As a reader, you may not have thought about trying to write a book yourself, but if you have, and you have a particular interest in medicine, then now is your chance.

We are specifically looking for new writers to join our established team of authors who write Medical Romances. Guidelines are available for this list, and we would be happy to send them to you.

Please mark the outside of your envelope 'Medical' to help speed our response, and we would be most grateful if you could include a stamped self-addressed envelope, size approximately $9\frac{1}{4}''$ x $4\frac{3}{4}''$, sent to the address below.

We look forward to hearing from you.

Editorial Department,
Mills & Boon Limited,
Eton House,
18-24 Paradise Road,
Richmond, Surrey,
TW9 1SR.

THE COMPELLING AND UNFORGETTABLE SAGA OF THE CALVERT FAMILY

April	August	November
£2.95	£3.50	£3.50

From the American Civil War to the outbreak of World War I, this sweeping historical romance trilogy depicts three generations of the formidable and captivating Calvert women – Sarah, Elizabeth and Catherine.

The ravages of war, the continued divide of North and South, success and failure, drive them all to discover an inner strength which proves they are true Calverts.

Top author Maura Seger weaves passion, pride, ambition and love into each story, to create a set of magnificent and unforgettable novels.

W●RLDWIDE

COMING SOON FROM MILLS & BOON!

Your chance to win the fabulous

VAUXHALL ASTRA MERIT 1.2 5-DOOR

Plus

2000 RUNNER UP PRIZES OF WEEKEND BREAKS & CLASSIC LOVE SONGS ON CASSETTE

♥ **SEE MILLS & BOON BOOKS** ♥
THROUGHOUT JULY & AUGUST FOR DETAILS!

Offer available through Boots, Martins, John Menzies, WH Smith, Woolworths and all good paperback stockists in the UK, Eire and Overseas.

THE IDEAL TONIC

Over the past year, we have listened carefully to readers' comments, and so, in August, Mills & Boon are launching a *new look* Doctor-Nurse series – MEDICAL ROMANCES.

There will still be three books every month from a wide selection of your favourite authors. As a special bonus, the three books in August will have a special offer price of **ONLY** 99p each.

So don't miss out on this chance to get a real insight into the fast-moving and varied world of modern medicine, which gives such a unique background to drama, emotions – and romance!